THE MIGHTY
ARE BACK!

A novel by Jordan Horowitz
Based on the motion picture from Walt Disney Pictures
Co-Producers Steven Brill and Salli Newman
Executive Producer Doug Claybourne
Based on characters created by Steven Brill
Based on the screenplay written by Steven Brill
Produced by Jordan Kerner and Jon Avnet
Directed by Sam Weisman

DISNEP
PRESS

NEW YORK

Copyright © 1994 by The Walt Disney Company.
All rights reserved. No part of this book may be used or reproduced
in any manner whatsoever
without written permission from the publisher.
Printed and bound in the United States of America.
For information address Disney Press,
114 Fifth Avenue, New York, New York 10011.
The stories, characters, and/or incidents in this publication
are entirely fictional.

1   3   5   7   9   10   8   6   4   2

Library of Congress Catalog Card Number: 93-73577

ISBN: 1-56282-692-1

D2

THE MIGHTY DUCKS ARE BACK!

1

BOMBAY OUT

Gordon Bombay, age thirty, felt like he was ninety. He sat hunched over on the bench behind the boards of the Duluth, Minnesota, ice hockey rink, his chest heaving.

He was gasping for breath. Alongside him sat his teammates. He looked at them. They were all half his age and barely out of high school. They were tired from the heavy action of the first two periods as well, but their breath came more steadily and easily than his.

Gordon looked across the ice at the other team. They were a squad of eager nineteen year olds.

Was he one of them, he wondered? Did he have what they had—the determination to make it to the pros?

Gordon shook his head. He felt as if he could be their grandfather.

1

Coach Blake was furious. "Bombay," he roared, "if you don't pick up your game, you're out of here! I'll give the roster spot to someone with a future!"

Gordon leaned his head back and sighed. He wondered if it hadn't been a mistake not going back to his old law firm to ask for his job back. What was he doing trying out with a minor league hockey team at his age? True, he hated the work at the law firm, but he was good at it. Playing professional hockey had been his only dream since he was a little kid. Gordon shook his head. He knew he couldn't go back to the law firm.

The year before, he had taken over as coach of a ragtag bunch of peewee hockey players who were so awful they could hardly skate in a straight line. But with a lot of practice and hard work, they surprised everyone—themselves included—by going all the way and winning the state hockey championship.

Gordon smiled. It was then that he had decided he had to take a shot at his dream, too. Win or lose.

The buzzer sounded, and Gordon vaulted over the railing onto the ice.

Miles away, in the back room of a neighborhood skate shop in St. Paul, Minnesota, thirteen-year-old Charlie Conway was listening to the Waves minor league hockey game on the radio. An older man sat at a work table, resharpening a pair of worn skates.

"Blake sends out the Bombay line," the announcer's voice crackled over the radio. Charlie fiddled with the tuner until the voice came through clearly. *"I'll tell ya, Bombay is really showing his age tonight. There's just no substitute for youth in this game. Great hands, but . . ."*

"Shut up and call the game," Charlie snapped. "I hate commentators," he told the older man. "They don't know what they're talking about."

"They don't know Gordon Bombay," Jan replied calmly.

Gordon leaned over and found himself nose to nose with a giant kid from the opposing team. It was the face-off. Gordon looked through his opponent's face guard and stared into the kid's face. He knew this guy. Norbert. Better known as the Wall.

"You ain't getting around me, Grandpa," said Norbert.

"I don't intend to . . . Son," Gordon replied with a curl of his upper lip.

The ref dropped the puck.

BAM! Gordon crashed into Norbert's chest. The surprise move worked. Norbert toppled. Gordon scraped the ice with his stick, slid the puck past

Norbert, and raced toward the goal. Then it was one, two, three—the triple deke—and whack! Gordon rammed the puck past the goalie and into the back of the net.

"That's his famous triple deke!" the announcer shouted over the radio in St. Paul. Charlie and Jan slapped their palms together in a victorious high five. *"What a move! What heart! Don't count this Bombay out!"*

"That's right," Charlie shouted at the radio. "He's a Duck!"

"Boy, he humiliated Norbert on the face-off," continued the announcer. *"Norbert is steaming as Bombay pumps his fist and embraces his teammates."*

Jan returned to his work. "Be careful, Gordon," Jan muttered softly to himself.

Seconds later Gordon Bombay was back on the ice. He had the puck and was sweeping it past Norbert. As he came up to the blue line, however, the puck wobbled and got caught between his skates.

Then WHAM!

Out of nowhere two defensemen hit him from both sides.

Gordon struggled to remain standing. But just then Norbert smashed straight into him and slashed his stick across Gordon's knees. Gordon doubled over and crumpled to the ice. He could feel the cartilage tear in his left kneecap.

A frightened hush came over the arena. Gordon tried to climb back onto his feet, but his leg gave way.

He fell to the ice again. It was the last thing Gordon remembered before passing out.

2

HOME TURF

On a rainy night two weeks later, Gordon Bombay limped off the Greyhound bus at the St. Paul station.

It was cold. Gordon hiked his equipment bag higher up on his shoulder and began limping down the street. A sports doctor had provided him with a cane, but the pain in his knee was still unbearable.

After a few minutes he noticed car lights spilling over him from behind. He turned around and saw a station wagon pulling up beside him. The window rolled down, and Gordon smiled when he recognized the driver.

"Welcome home, Gordon."

"Jan, how did you know I was coming back?" Gordon asked.

"Where else would you go? Get in."

"Hans couldn't make it?" inquired Gordon as he climbed into the wagon and threw his bag onto the backseat.

"That strudlehead," said Jan about his brother. "He went back to Scandinavia for the summer. Left me the shop to run by myself. He said he had to go home, visit Momma. She loves him more than you know. I don't care. You can have his bed. Welcome back. You look tired."

Gordon sighed. If only he knew how tired, Gordon thought.

SCREEEEECH!

Gordon bolted awake and practically leaped off the sofa bed at the sound of metal against metal. Then he remembered where he was. He was in a corner off the back room of Jan & Hans's Sports Shop.

Gordon pulled the curtain away from a window and saw that it was morning. Then he grabbed his cane and limped toward the scraping sound.

He thought he would find Jan working at the repair bench, but instead he saw a boy hunched over the sharpening blade. Sparks were flying all around him. The boy heard Gordon enter, and he shut the motor off and turned around.

It was Charlie Conway.

"Sorry," said Charlie. "Did I wake you?"

Gordon smiled. Charlie broke into a big grin. They gave each other a warm hug.

Just then Jan came in from the kitchen carrying a tray covered with bowls.

"For breakfast," Jan announced, "my specialty! Jan's hasen—"

"Hasenpfeffer and eggs!" Charlie and Gordon said together.

"I see you met my new apprentice," Jan said as he put the bowls of food down before them.

"Jan told me you did this job when you were my age," Charlie said to his old coach.

"I sure did." Gordon smiled. It was a warm memory. "Hope he pays you more than he paid me."

"You got PAID?" said Charlie.

"Eat, everyone!" said Jan, quickly changing the subject. "Before the hasenpfeffer gets cold!"

After breakfast Charlie went back to work at the repair table. Gordon found some framed photographs and newspaper clippings hanging on the wall behind the sales counter. Most of the clippings were yellowed with age. But in the dead center of them all was a newer, more freshly framed clipping. The headline proclaimed: MINNESOTA MIRACLE—DUCKS BEAT HAWKS!

"That was a good day," Gordon told Jan, pointing to the clipping.

Gordon glanced over at Charlie, who was hard

at work repairing a pair of skates. "Look at him," he said to Jan. "Wow, he's grown."

"They do that," said Jan, grinning. "Since his mother remarried he started spending a lot of time here. I had to hire him."

"I should have kept in touch more," sighed Gordon.

"You are here now," said Jan. "So, what is your plan? Have you talked to Ducksworth?"

"I'm a player, not a lawyer," said Gordon, recalling his old job at the law firm of Ducksworth, Saver and Gross.

"But your injury requires rest and time."

"Time is the one thing I don't have," explained Gordon. "I was this close to the NHL. I could taste it. I was in the game, Jan. I was alive."

Jan looked at Gordon. Gordon was clutching his cane tightly, trying to look as if he wasn't in pain.

"Have you thought about coaching?" asked Jan. "After all, you are the Minnesota Miracle Man. You still have the Ducks, in case you forgot."

"I'm Duck through and through, Jan," said Gordon. "But I can't make a living coaching peewee hockey, can I?"

"Where there is a way there must be a will," quipped Jan. "For example, my hockey suppliers tell me Team USA is still without a coach for the Junior Goodwill Games."

"Sounds great," Gordon groaned sarcastically.

"Give 'em a call for me, Jan. Tell 'em I'm available. I'm sure they'll be knocked out. I can sharpen their skates."

"Don't knock skate sharpening," Jan gently retorted. "It is a skill. My father taught—"

"I know, Jan. I know. It's a great skill, but I don't want to stay in this rinky-dink town, sharpening skates my whole life. Heck, even the North Stars moved. I want something better, too, Jan. Something bigger."

3

RETURN OF THE DUCKS

Jan eventually convinced Gordon to try his hand at skate sharpening. It had been years since Gordon worked the sharpener, and he had lost the touch. It was just one more frustrating thing for Gordon to deal with. But he had promised Jan that he would help out around the shop. At least for a while.

One afternoon, just as Gordon had finished the morning's load of sharpening, Jan entered the workroom and dropped an afternoon's worth of skates on the repair bench. Gordon sighed, exhausted just at the sight of them.

"You don't have to do them right now," said Jan. "We have customers. Go help them, then come back and do it."

Gordon scowled and trudged to the front of the store. A man in a very expensive business suit was trying out a hockey stick from the rack. He swung the stick and knocked down a display of pucks.

The man didn't look like much of an athlete.

"Can I help you?" asked Gordon.

The man clumsily replaced the pucks on their display table and returned the stick to the rack. Then he approached Gordon with a wide, toothy smile.

"You look even better in person," said the man.

"Thank you," said Gordon, a little confused.

"Don Tibbles," the man said, introducing himself. He held out his hand. Gordon shook it. "Senior vice president, Hendrix Hockey Apparel. How's the knee? I know a doctor in Los Angeles I want you to see; he's doing great things with baboon ligaments—"

"What exactly is it you want, Mr. Tibbles?" interrupted Gordon.

"*You,* Gordo," answered Tibbles. "I want the next coach of Team USA to be a household name. I want you to be synonymous with winning and winning to be synonymous with Hendrix. As the official sponsor of Team USA Hockey at the Junior Goodwill Games I am here to say welcome. Welcome. Is that how you always wear your hair?"

"Time out," said Gordon. Was this guy for real? "Did you say the next coach of Team USA? *I'm* the next coach?"

"Darned straight," said Tibbles with a flash of his teeth. "Jan has been pitching you for months. What you did with the Ducks was magic. Now we—Hendrix Hockey—the Junior Goodwill Games—your country—need that magic."

Gordon turned around and saw Jan standing in the doorway of the back room with a broad, knowing smile on his face.

"How did you do it, Jan?" asked Gordon.

"I have my ways."

Tibbles took a step closer to Gordon. "Go round up your Ducks, Gordo," he told him. "We've got a lot of work to do."

Within minutes Gordon was out the door.

Charlie Conway was in his bedroom struggling with his American history homework when he heard a strange noise outside his window. *Quaaaack!* Charlie smiled and ran to the window. Gordon Bombay was sending out a duck call. When they saw each other they both broke into huge grins.

Gordon explained to Charlie about the offer from Hendrix Hockey Apparel and asked Charlie to round up the team. Charlie didn't have much trouble finding seven of the original Ducks.

Jesse Hall was playing roller hockey on a basketball court not far from his house. At a mall downtown they found Les Averman at his job tearing tickets at a movie theater. He happily agreed to play. Connie Cascardi and Guy Germaine were Rollerblading in the park when the boys tracked them down. Connie wanted to play, too. Guy wanted to be anywhere Connie was.

Goldberg was working at his dad's delicatessen. The kids pressed their faces against the window, and Charlie blew on his duck call. Goldberg smiled, gave his father a quick look, then ran out before his father could stop him. Of course, he did manage to stop just long enough to grab the leftovers of a fat pastrami sandwich on his way out.

Adam Banks was practicing his stickhandling in his driveway in front of his house. The idea of playing international hockey made his eyes grow as wide as saucers. It didn't take much effort to convince Adam to play. Hockey was his life.

There was one more player to find before the Ducks would be complete. In the park the kids burst out laughing when they saw three Hawks players floating in a canoe on the lake . . . in their underwear. The Ducks had beaten the Hawks to win the championship the year before. Only one person was big enough to take on three Hawks. Fulton Reed.

The Ducks were back!

4

NEW DUCKS

"Welcome back, Ducks," said Gordon, beaming. "I sure missed you guys."

The seven Ducks cheered. They were grouped around Gordon in front of the old District Five band box.

"All right now," said Gordon. "Who's ready to fly?"

The kids cheered again. "COACH!" they shouted in unison. "COACH! COACH! COACH! COACH!"

While they cheered, a white limousine pulled up behind them. The sunroof of the car opened, and up popped Don Tibbles.

"Hi," he said, greeting the Ducks, and began to pass out his business card. "Don Tibbles. Hendrix Hockey Apparel. Your official sponsor. Good to see you all. You look like a fine bunch. Not so close to the car, please. Gordon, step into my office."

Tibbles dropped back into the car and opened the back door. The Ducks swarmed around trying to get a peek at the inside of the limo.

"Adults only," said Tibbles as he motioned for Gordon. "You kids practice your puck sticking."

"That's puck handling," smirked Gordon as he entered the limo.

Tibbles closed the door behind them. Gordon settled into the backseat. The plush leather interior with the built-in TV and bar reminded him of the kind of car he used to drive when he was working as a highly paid lawyer.

"Nice," Gordon commented. "I used to ride in one of these, a little smaller though. How many channels does your TV get?"

"How many do you want?" quipped Tibbles. "Listen. Before we head to Taylor Falls, we have to talk about your endorsements."

"Endorsements? I'm just a coach."

"Just a coach?" Tibbles sounded surprised. "Is Pat Riley just a coach? Chuck Daly? Ditka?"

"Ditka's out of a job," Gordon said sarcastically.

"Go down to the bank and you'll see him laughing his head off. Listen, Gordon. Coaches today have images. Images mean dollars. I sell you, you sell the sport. We both get rich. How's that sound?"

Gordon wasn't sure. "I've got nothing against making money," he said thoughtfully.

16

"There is so much more to life, I know," Tibbles said, finishing his thought for him. "You do well at the Goodwill Games and the sky's the limit. With your legal experience you could move into the front office. Want to coach in the pros? Go from the Games to the minors right into the NHL? Think you can still play? I can get you a priority tryout with any team in the league. It can be easy if you know the right people. Fortunately for you, I happen to be one of those people."

Tibbles shoved a contract into Gordon's hands. "Look these over when you get a minute," he urged. "I'll see you tomorrow in Taylor Falls."

"Why are we going there?" asked Gordon.

"Team USA training facility—two hours north, total boondocks, supposed to limit distractions," explained Tibbles as he turned the knob to open the back door. "We train for two weeks, then straight to L.A., my kind of town."

Tibbles tried to open the door but couldn't budge it. He pushed a little harder, opening it a crack. A hand pushed through, then an arm, then a face.

It was Goldberg. Behind him were the rest of the Ducks. They were trying a full frontal assault on the limo.

Tibbles pushed Gordon out of the car and into the flock of kids. It was the only way he could shut the door and prevent the invasion.

Gordon grinned as he watched the limo peel

away from the band box. Around him were his Ducks. They were all fired up, excited about the prospect of going international and playing against the world.

He looked down at the contract that was folded in his hands. His thoughts shifted abruptly to the pain in his knee.

Maybe there *was* a future for him in hockey, after all.

Late the following week special arrangements had been made to let the kids out of school until the conclusion of the Goodwill Games.

"We train hard for two weeks, then it's straight to Los Angeles," Gordon explained to the Ducks on the bus ride to Taylor Falls. "Tibbles and the Goodwill Committee have scoured the country, and they're filling in our roster with some new players. I expect you all to welcome them with open arms."

Hours later the Ducks filed out of the bus and followed Gordon into the Minnetonka arena where they would be training. By the time they settled in and suited up for their first practice, five kids were already on the ice warming up. The Ducks watched them warily.

"Gordo! Kids!" It was Tibbles, dressed in designer sweats, a whistle hanging around his neck. He was standing on the side bench. "Welcome to the Team USA training facility. I was just putting the new guys through some paces and—"

"I'd prefer it if you left the coaching to me," said Gordon as he approached Tibbles.

Tibbles smiled graciously. "Take-charge. Assured." He smiled and winked. "I like it."

"I'm glad," said Gordon. "Now please get down from there and tell me about my new kids."

Tibbles pointed to each of the new team members as he described them.

"Luis Mendoza, from our Miami club," he said. "Clocked him at one-point-one-nine seconds blue line to blue line. One little problem, though . . ."

Luis tried to stop once he passed the blue line but couldn't. He slammed hard into the board.

Tibbles sighed. "Luis *does* have a little trouble stopping."

Next, a tall, lanky boy skated past Gordon. "YEEEHAWWW!" he yelled. "How's everyone?" he called out to the Ducks. "Y'all ready to play some puck?"

"That's Dwayne Robertson," Tibbles told Gordon. "Best puck handler I've ever seen."

"You mean at his age?" asked Gordon.

"No," answered Tibbles. "I don't."

Dwayne danced across the ice, handling the puck deftly.

Tibbles pointed to the goalie protecting the net.

"Julie 'the Cat' Gaffney," said Tibbles. "She won

the state championship for Maine three years in a row."

"We have a goalie," said Gordon. "Goldberg."

Gordon watched spellbound as Dwayne slammed the puck toward the net. Julie nimbly snapped the puck out of midair like a cat swatting at a fly.

"Then again, we do need a backup," Gordon said, impressed.

A skater in a pair of jet black figure skates glided onto the ice.

"Isn't that the kid from the Olympics?" Gordon asked Tibbles. "The Korean figure skater?"

"Ken Wu," answered Tibbles. "What can I say? I convinced him hockey held more of a future. He picked up a stick, and now no one can touch him."

Ken skated gracefully toward the Ducks, then jumped around a startled Fulton.

"Hey, you can't do that!" shouted Fulton.

"Yes I can," laughed Ken. "Anytime, anyplace." He skated backward, then did a pirouette, narrowly missing bumping into another of the new players as he came to a full stop.

The player was about twice Ken's size and taller than any of the Ducks. He had a bandanna around his head, and his Walkman was on full blast. He was playing air guitar as he lumbered past the Ducks.

"He can hardly skate," Gordon said. "He's a goon."

"Portman?" said Tibbles. "I believe he's what you'd call an enforcer. And when you play Team Iceland, you're gonna need him."

Charlie skated out onto the ice to scrimmage and immediately went for the puck. Portman cornered him and lifted him off the ground with one hand. Then he hung him by his jersey on a corner of the Plexiglas window above the boards.

Then Portman calmly skated away with the puck.

Upset over the bullying play, Adam Banks skated over to Portman. "You can't do that!" he complained.

Portman took Banks by the arm, twirled him around, and sent him twirling across the ice.

Fulton charged up from behind Portman and pulled his headphones off. Portman whirled around.

"Hey," he shouted at Fulton. "That was the best part of the song, DUDE!"

That was it. Both boys started pushing one another. They growled and they grumbled like two dogs ready to fight. Before long, all the old Ducks began circling their new teammates, staring each other down as they moved, each side challenging the other.

"Everyone freeze!" ordered Gordon.

The kids obeyed.

"You are here to play hockey," he reminded the

kids. "We're Team USA. You represent your country now. That means you play hard and you play fair. I want you to—"

"Be all you can be!" added Tibbles, who was becoming fired up by Gordon's enthusiasm. "Go for the gold! Come on! YES!"

Gordon threw Tibbles a look. Tibbles shrugged apologetically and backed away.

"Leave the egos at the door," Gordon continued. "We're all on the same team. Okay, let's start with a scrimmage."

A whistle blew. It was Tibbles again.

"You heard him," Tibbles shouted. "It's do or die! Scrimmage! Let's—" Once again he was cut off by Gordon's cold stare.

"You know what?" Tibbles said sheepishly. "I just remembered I have to go meet Ms. MacKay, the team tutor."

Tibbles tried to slip away. Before he could, Gordon held out his hand. Tibbles looked down at his whistle. Reluctantly he removed it from around his neck and returned it to Gordon.

"You'll get it back at the end of the school term," said Gordon, and the kids all laughed.

Gordon broke the squad into two sides. Jesse faced off against Dwayne. Dwayne stole the puck by tapping it through Jesse's legs. It was too fast a move for Jesse, and he slipped and fell on his backside.

Next Fulton came barreling across the ice. He knocked Dwayne down and leaned in to take the puck, but not before Portman appeared out of nowhere and knocked Fulton down. The scrimmage went downhill from there.

To Gordon it looked as if the old Ducks were out of shape. They were easily tired and gulped greedily for air.

"Haven't you been training in the off-season?" Gordon shouted as Averman skated by, huffing and puffing.

"I knew we forgot something!" quipped Averman.

Charlie went after the puck, and he slipped and fell on his face. Dwayne recovered the puck and passed it to Ken, who passed it to Luis, who picked up speed as he headed toward the net.

There was just one problem: he couldn't stop. He slammed into Goldberg at the net, and both players went tumbling head over heels.

Gordon took Goldberg off the ice to recover and replaced him with Julie, the new goalie. Jesse tried to shoot the puck past her, but she made a save with calculated precision and agility.

Banks tried his luck. He picked off an errant pass near his own blue line and skillfully began to guide the puck down the ice toward the net. Suddenly he picked up speed and lunged for the face-off circle to Julie's right. At the last second he veered back to the center and smashed the puck straight at the net. Julie was caught off guard. He scored.

Banks swerved full around once, then looked back. He and Julie stared at one another.

Later Fulton got hold of the puck and started to wind up for one of his patented cannon shots. Averman, Jesse, Charlie, Guy, and Connie skated clear. They knew how deadly Fulton's slap shot could be. Portman, however, stood placidly by, on the ice, watching Fulton.

SMASH!

The puck went screaming through the air. Portman ducked just in time. So did Luis, Dwayne, and Ken.

The puck smashed into the goalpost and ricocheted like a bullet into the stands. At that very moment, Tibbles was escorting an attractive dark-haired woman into the arena.

"You're gonna love these tykes," he told the woman. "Half are from various parts of the U.S. Real ringers. The other half are Bombay's old team called—"

"DUCK!" the woman screamed as she caught sight of the wayward puck.

Tibbles smiled. "That's right," he said. "The Ducks."

He turned.

It was the last thing he remembered doing.

5

THE TUTOR AND THE COACH

Tibbles regained consciousness. Gordon helped him to a bleacher seat.

"He'll be okay," the woman told Gordon. "Just keep an eye on him."

Gordon looked at the woman. She smiled at him.

"Hi," she said. "I'm sorry. He didn't get a chance to introduce us. I'm Michele MacKay, the team's tutor."

"Yes, hi," replied Gordon. "I'm Gordon Bombay, their coach. Team, this is Ms. MacKay."

"I don't need no school!" shouted Portman.

"Yeah," agreed Banks. "Who said we need a tutor?"

"The Minnesota State Department of Welfare," answered Ms. MacKay. "I have to teach you for three hours, Monday through Friday."

"It's the rules, guys. Gotta live by 'em," agreed

Gordon. The Ducks let out a collective groan. Gordon looked at his watch. "I need them for another hour, Ms. MacKay, but you can have them, say, at two thirty."

"Oh no," said the tutor. "Maybe I wasn't clear. The hours for instruction must be between ten and three. Sorry, it's the rules, Mr. Bombay. Gotta live by 'em."

Goldberg stepped forward and placed a hand on Ms. MacKay's shoulders. "Ms. MacKay," he said, sounding very serious. "We're America's team. Shouldn't we just be concentrating on hockey? May I suggest optional school attendance?"

"That's not a bad idea," replied Ms. MacKay. "School will be optional."

The kids cheered.

"However," Ms. MacKay continued, "should you not attend, you will not be eligible to play."

Now the kids groaned.

"I'll be required to travel with you to Los Angeles," Ms. MacKay explained to Gordon. "Their education should never be interrupted. Don't you agree?"

"Absolutely," replied Gordon. The kids had finished practice, and Gordon was on the bench working with the playbook. "So, you can teach all the subjects? You must be smart."

"I am," said Ms. MacKay with confidence.

"How'd you get that way?"

"Good teachers and good books."

"Hey. I just finished a good book today," said Gordon. "Three hundred and fifty pages long. That's a lot of coloring, let me tell ya." Gordon laughed, but Ms. MacKay did not. She didn't think it was funny. "Joke," prompted Gordon. "That was a joke."

"I know," Ms. MacKay said flatly.

"Are you a big hockey fan?"

Ms. MacKay frowned. "No. I really don't care a great deal about sports."

"I could teach you," Gordon offered. "Once you know how the game is played it—"

"I know how sports are played," Ms. MacKay snapped. "I grew up with three brothers. Let's just say I'm not a big hockey fan. It can be a little, I don't know, *barbaric*. Toothless guys with sticks."

Gordon gave Ms. MacKay a critical, disapproving look.

"It's the most beautiful sport in the world," Gordon said.

Ms. MacKay shrugged. "Opinions vary. I'm just here to tutor the kids and provide them with some adult supervision."

"My kids are well behaved and responsible," said Gordon. "I'm capable of providing them with all the adult supervision they need."

Just then they were interrupted by the roar of

a motor. Gordon and Michele turned. The Zamboni ice machine crashed into the boards and belched a thick cloud of dark smoke.

Then they saw Fulton, Guy, and Jesse emerge from the smoke. They jumped off the machine, coughing and waving their arms.

"Don't worry," Fulton cracked. "We're okay!" The three boys headed nonchalantly into the locker room.

Gordon turned a sheepish grin toward Ms. MacKay.

"I'm sorry," Ms. MacKay said. "You were saying something about well-behaved boys?"

Gordon's face turned red.

The Ducks were gathered for class in a makeshift classroom in the arena. They sat scattered among folding chairs and groaned as Ms. MacKay wrote out geometry equations on a portable rolling blackboard.

Their minds were definitely not on mathematics.

"You guys can't just come here and be Ducks," Jesse whispered sharply to Portman, who was sitting in the row in front of him. "We earned our wings."

"Ducks stink," scoffed Portman. "I play for me."

Guy was sitting next to Luis. Luis was throwing

smiles at Connie, just as he had been doing all afternoon. And what was worse, Connie was smiling back. Guy didn't like it.

"Hey, speedy, quit scammin' my babe," he warned Luis.

"The name's Luis. Sorry, amigo. Didn't mean to ruffle your Duck feathers."

Ms. MacKay looked up from the blackboard. "Okay," she called out. "Who can tell me what an isosceles triangle is? Dwayne?"

The kids snickered. Meanwhile, Guy saw Connie throw another smile at Luis.

"I saw that, Connie," said Guy angrily.

"You don't own me," Connie retorted.

Luis smiled. "She's right, my friend," he said smugly.

"I'm not your friend!" shouted Guy.

"Good," said Luis. "Then I won't feel so bad when Connie and I are together."

"Boys, that is enough!" ordered Ms. MacKay. "I mean it. Okay now. Can anyone tell me what an isosce—"

"NOBODY MOVES!"

All heads turned. It was Portman. "My Nirvana tape is missing!" He turned to face Fulton, in the seat beside him. "You snagged it, didn't you?"

"Yeah, here it is," said Fulton flippantly. He threw a roll of black hockey tape at Portman. Portman ducked. The tape was intercepted, a few seats over, by Julie. Then Portman and Fulton jumped to their feet and began shoving each other.

At the same time, Guy and Luis began poking one another, challenging each other to a fight over Connie. Connie was trying to break it up.

Within seconds wads of crumpled paper hurtled across the seats like snowballs. Jesse, Goldberg, Banks, and Averman had begun a paper-wad war with Dwayne, Ken, and Julie.

Things were getting out of hand.

"Stop it, class!" shouted Ms. MacKay as a paper ball whizzed past her shoulder and hit the blackboard. "Class! Team USA!"

"Cool it, guys!" shouted Charlie, who was immediately pummeled with a barrage of paper balls.

Gordon had been watching the scene from the locker-room doorway. He walked casually over to the blackboard.

"Need any help, adult supervision—wise?" he quipped to Ms. MacKay. She shot him an angry stare.

Gordon smiled knowingly. "You need to treat the children with patience and understanding," he suggested. Then he took a step toward the unruly class and blasted his whistle.

"ALL RIGHT—KNOCK IT OFF AND SIT DOWN!" he shouted.

There was instant silence as the kids returned to their seats.

Ms. MacKay leaned over to Gordon. "Patience and understanding?" she reminded him.

Gordon grinned. "Patience, understanding," he began, "and a loud whistle."

6

THE MIGHTY...TEAM USA?

The following day training began in earnest. Gordon gathered the Ducks, or Team USA, as they were now called, onto the rink. He hobbled them together into a line, then tied them to each other with packing cord.

"This is more crowded than a truckload of goats," complained Dwayne.

"Yeech," screeched Averman. "Somebody licked me!"

Gordon walked back and forth in front of the team.

"I can't think of any way to make it clearer. You are a team. To win this thing, we're going to have to work as one. Now be ONE—skate!"

The kids started moving, but in different directions. The rope yanked them back, and they toppled over each other into a confused heap.

"Everyone goes their own way, everyone falls down," explained Gordon. "Now get up and do it again."

After several tries Team USA was able to move slowly, very slowly, in the same direction. When he was satisfied that they were working as a team again, Gordon untied them and handed the rope to Dwayne.

"Okay, Rancher Dwayne," he said. "Go round me up some stray calf." Then he promised double dessert to the last player left standing.

The kids took off, free-skating in all directions. Dwayne smiled as he tied the rope into a lariat and took off after them. He twirled the rope and easily lassoed Goldberg first. Dwayne guided Goldberg off the ice as if he were bringing a cow in for branding.

Dwayne returned to the ice and began lassoing players as though he were scoring points in a video game. Connie, Luis, Averman, Jesse, Julie, Charlie. One by one Dwayne lassoed them and took them off the ice.

There were only three players left: Ken, Banks, and Portman.

Ken tried to twirl away but was caught by Dwayne's loop in midpirouette. Upon seeing this, Portman decided he had finally had enough. He went on the offensive. He charged Dwayne like a mad bull. Dwayne fled across the ice, but when he was a safe distance away he did a sharp about-face. Portman shot past Dwayne and never saw the rope until it circled around his waist and jerked him to a dead stop.

The workout was over.

Everyone was watching Adam Banks start in on his second cup of pudding when Tibbles entered the dining hall. He was pushing a cloth-covered cart into the center of the room.

"I know you athletes need your food," he said, calling for their attention, "but let me interrupt you for a moment. Winning the Junior Goodwill Games is more than just a victory. It's a chance to be immortalized in a time-honored tradition."

With that, Tibbles ceremoniously whipped the cloth off the cart to reveal a huge, oversize box of USA Crunch cereal. Plastered across the front of the box was a photograph of Gordon and the team.

Gordon couldn't help but smile.

"Hey, that's us!" shouted Dwayne.

"Today it's a cereal box," said Tibbles. "Tomorrow it's video games, action figures, lunch boxes. Maybe they'll even make a movie about you. Stranger things have happened. Now, just so everybody knows who you are, put away those old Duck jerseys because from now on you'll be wearing these!"

Tibbles opened the cereal box and pulled out a

bunch of beautiful red-white-and-blue warm-up suits with Team USA embroidered across the front and Hendrix sewn down the sleeves.

Portman, Luis, Julie, Dwayne, and Ken scrambled for their new uniforms. But the old Ducks hesitated. They didn't like the idea of giving up the Mighty Ducks.

"This stuff has Hendrix written all over it," muttered Charlie.

"They're our sponsors, Charlie," Gordon explained.

"So what?" Charlie replied. "Why can't we be USA Ducks or at least keep our Duck colors?"

"Charlie, it's business stuff," Gordon said. The fact was, he explained, they weren't the Ducks anymore. They were a new team. Team USA.

Seeing his picture on the front of the cereal box, Gordon knew he wasn't the coach of the Ducks anymore, either. He was the coach of Team USA.

As far as he was concerned, the Ducks were history.

7

A TEAM IS BORN

That afternoon Ms. MacKay arranged to hold class outdoors, along the river. By getting the kids away from the rink for a few hours, she hoped to get their minds off hockey and onto their studies.

It worked. The kids were different away from practice. They seemed less serious and more like kids.

"We were talking about history," Ms. MacKay reminded the class. "How many of you knew that the first Olympic Games were held in Greece?"

"Must have been pretty slippery," quipped Averman. Everyone groaned at the bad joke.

Ms. MacKay continued. "Ancient Greece was the beginning of Western civilization. Medicine, architecture, math, along with the idea of bringing the world together in sporting competition, all came from this place and time."

"What about the gladiators?" asked Portman.

"That was ancient Rome, Dean," explained Ms. MacKay. "And gladiators were more like professional athletes. In Greece they didn't have professional sports or cereal boxes. So the athletes competed for another reason. Anybody?"

"Pride," offered Charlie.

Ms. MacKay nodded. "That's right," she said with a smile. "The various city-states waved their flags and wore their home colors proudly."

Ms. MacKay felt energized by the way the kids were participating. She looked up and saw Gordon stroll to a stop behind the group.

"Did America always dominate?" asked Fulton.

"Well, no," explained Ms. MacKay. "America wasn't around back then. Don't forget that America, compared to other countries, is still young, still forming an identity. America is like a teenager, like you."

"Like us?" asked Jesse, his brow twisted quizzically.

"You bet," said Ms. MacKay. "A little awkward at times, but always right there on the verge of greatness."

The kids smiled at that comparison. Gordon was smiling as well.

After class Gordon and the team worked out on some hilly roads. They put on their Rollerblades, knee pads, wrist guards, and helmets. Then Gordon took off in a golf cart and ordered the team to follow him into the hills on their skates.

"Left, right, left, right!" Gordon shouted like a drill sergeant. "Minnesota for a climate not-so-colda! Now we're goin' all the way! We're goin' for the . . ."

"GOLD!" the team answered in unison as they huffed and struggled to keep up.

"I said we're goin' all the way," continued Gordon. " 'Cause we're . . ."

"TEAM USA!" answered the kids.

Just then Portman lost his footing and fell. Fulton, who was just in front of him, turned. He reached out his hand to help Portman up. Portman hesitated. The two boys stared at each other for a moment.

Finally Portman grabbed Fulton's hand and let himself be pulled up.

Thirty minutes later Gordon led the kids to the docks. While the kids cooled down in the breeze that drifted from the lake, he and Ms. MacKay took a walk along the shore.

"All in all, they're a good bunch," commented Ms. MacKay.

"You're great with them," Gordon told her. Ms.

MacKay blushed. "I really mean that. I hardly remember any of my teachers. I wish I had you as a teacher growing up."

"You never had any good teachers?"

"Well, my dad," said Gordon somberly. "He taught me how to play hockey. He taught me about life."

"That's nice," she said. "My mom was a big influence on me. She was a teacher. Still is, actually. She's been at the same school for thirty years."

"Where?"

"Duluth County High."

"The Fighting Tangerines?"

"Wolverines," Michele corrected him.

"I know," said Gordon. "We called them the Tangerines. We played them in football."

"I know," said Michele. "I was a cheerleader."

Gordon smiled.

"Don't you say a word," Michele warned him. They both began laughing.

Suddenly the sound of a motor being revved came from behind them. Gordon and Ms. MacKay whipped around just in time to see Fulton, Guy, and Jesse driving the golf cart. It was out of control and heading right for them. Gordon quickly pulled Ms. MacKay out of the way.

CRASH! SPLASH!

The cart plunged off the dock and into the shallow water. Gordon, Ms. MacKay, and the rest of the kids ran to the dock. The three boys were still sitting in the golf cart.

"Someone has to teach those kids how to drive," Ms. MacKay suggested.

Gordon giggled. Then she laughed. Soon all of Team USA was rolling over with laughter.

8

THE ONLY WAY BACK
INTO THE GAME

A week later the team landed at Los Angeles International Airport. They were greeted by Tibbles and a special bus with the words Team USA and Hendrix Apparel emblazoned across its sides.

Before they went to the hotel, however, they detoured through Beverly Hills. Expensive sports cars raced past them on Rodeo Drive. And on every street corner, peddlers hawked maps to the homes of the stars.

Gordon and the kids were dazzled.

Finally the bus pulled into the Los Angeles Coliseum, where a special media event had been scheduled to introduce all the teams participating in the Junior Goodwill Games.

Through the windows of the bus, Gordon and the kids saw a banner stretched out across the road.

Los Angeles—Junior Goodwill Games Welcomes You.

Just outside the main entrance to the coliseum were dozens of local television news vans with satellite dishes on them.

Gordon, Michele, and the team climbed out of the bus and followed Tibbles into the coliseum. The stadium was thronging with all the activity of a major convention. There were welcome booths, administration tents, banners, and flags everywhere.

Two teenage girls excitedly approached Luis and Dwayne and asked them to sign their programs. It didn't take long for the boys to get into the swing of things. Soon they were signing programs and talking to fans like old pros.

Portman had just finished signing a program when he looked up to see a boy his own age dressed in oversize jeans and a hooded sweat jacket staring at him.

"You want an autograph?" asked Portman.

The kid shook his head disgustedly and walked away.

Tibbles ushered Gordon and his team into the Team USA press tent. The tent was ablaze with TV lights. Immediately a mob of reporters and photographers descended on Gordon. Tibbles tried holding the reporters back and guided Gordon to the center of the tent, where an attractive woman in a business suit waited.

"Gordon," said Tibbles, "this is Marcy Hendrix, president of Hendrix Hockey Apparel."

Gordon held out his hand. Ms. Hendrix ignored the gesture. Instead, she looked him up and down.

"You have nice skin," she said bluntly. She had not meant it as a compliment.

"Thank you," replied Gordon uncertainly.

Ms. Hendrix turned abruptly to Tibbles. "Make sure you get pictures of him with the bear." Then she pushed past the reporters and out of the tent.

Suddenly Gordon felt a tap on his shoulder. He turned around, expecting to see a reporter. Instead, he saw a six-foot-tall white furry polar bear standing straight up on its hind legs. It was the team mascot. The bear threw its paw around his shoulder.

Gordon blinked as dozens of flashbulbs went off around the tent. Tibbles stepped forward.

"Here they are," he announced proudly to the reporters as they shoved their microphones and tape recorders forward. "TEAM USA HOCKEY." He slapped Gordon on the back. "And here's the man chosen to lead them to the gold. Gordon Bombay, formerly of the Mighty Ducks, now the youngest man ever to coach Team USA." He leaned and whispered, "Big smile, Gordo."

"Gordo" smiled as more flashbulbs went off.

A reporter shoved her microphone into Gordon's face. "Most people think it would be a miracle for Team USA to grab a bronze," she said, "let alone a gold. What do you say?"

Jesse jumped in front of Gordon. "I say most people are fools," he shouted. "Hi, Mom! Hi, Dad!"

Another reporter stepped toward Gordon with his microphone.

"The Vikings from Team Iceland are the heavy favorites," he said. "Their coach all but guaranteed victory. How will you handle them?"

There was a momentary pause. Tibbles watched Gordon expectantly. Gordon pulled the microphone closer to his face.

"We'll handle them the old-fashioned way," Gordon promised. "Hard work. We'll work hard, we'll play hard, and we'll stick together. Iceland might be tough, but we're Team USA and *we're* going all the way!"

The kids cheered. Tibbles threw Gordon an energetic thumbs-up.

"Team USA is going down!"

A silence came over the room. All eyes turned to the back of the tent. A tall man with slicked-back hair was standing alone at the back of the tent. He was wearing a Vikings windbreaker.

"Team USA is going down," he repeated for the reporters. "That is where they are going."

Before the reporters could reach him for further comment, he stormed out of the tent.

"That's just the Icelandic coach, Stansson," Tibbles whispered to Gordon. "A little high-strung."

Gordon raised an eyebrow. "Stansson?" he asked. "From the NHL? Wolf 'the Dentist' Stansson is coaching? You didn't tell me that."

"That guy was a dentist?" asked Ken.

"That was his nickname," Charlie explained to the others. "He played pro for one year. He collected more teeth than goals. He even punched his own coach. They ran him out of the league and the country."

"I heard he went home," said Julie, "but lost his eligibility to play on the Olympic team."

Charlie shrugged. "I guess coaching is his only way back into the game," he said.

Gordon overheard what Charlie said. Maybe he and Stansson had something in common, after all.

9

OPENING CEREMONIES

The Ducks may have been exhausted after their first day in Los Angeles, but they were also exhilarated. All the attention—the reporters, the cameras, the fans—had made them feel important. They were being treated like royalty. Now they looked forward to a luxurious night's sleep in a four-star hotel, complete with pool, sauna, TV, VCR, and room service.

But their happy expressions dropped as they were led to their accommodations by a representative of Hendrix Apparel. It was a dormitory building in an isolated section of a local college campus. The building was low and rectangular and looked something like a gray shoe box with windows. Inside, it wasn't any more luxurious. The rooms were dark, with thick cement walls and bunk beds with mattresses that sagged in the middle.

So much for the royal treatment, the kids thought.

Meanwhile, miles away on Malibu Beach, Gordon Bombay followed Don Tibbles into the ultra-modern two-story beach house that would be *his* accommodations. Gordon had only seen this kind of a place on "Lifestyles of the Rich and Famous," but now he was in one. And he was being treated like he was rich and famous, too. Still, he wondered if he shouldn't be spending the night with the team, wherever they were.

Then Tibbles flung open the drapes. Gordon had never seen so much ocean. Or any ocean, for that matter. He opened the sliding glass door on the porch, and a wave of cool sea air brushed over Gordon's face. Minutes later Gordon found himself facedown on a massage table, the gentle hands of a professional masseuse kneading out the knots in his back. Tibbles—and Hendrix—had arranged for it all.

Gordon smiled. "Well," he told himself, "it's not like the team needs me twenty-four hours a day."

When Tibbles barged into Gordon's room late the next morning, he woke him from the most peaceful night of his life. If they didn't hurry, Tibbles warned him, they'd be late for the opening ceremonies.

"Where's *our* coach?" Luis asked that morning. All the teams were assembled, and the introductory ceremonies had already begun.

"Must be doing *business stuff*," scowled Charlie. He adjusted himself in his new Team USA uniform. It was tight and uncomfortable. He wished he could be wearing his old Ducks uniform.

Just then Gordon and Tibbles arrived. Gordon was still adjusting his tie when a tall, fair-haired woman approached him.

"I can help tie you," she said. She spoke with a Scandinavian accent.

Gordon was too stunned by the woman's beauty to object. He let her tie his tie.

"I'm Gordon," he said.

"I am Marria," she said.

A wide shadow fell over them. Gordon looked up. The huge form of Coach Wolf Stansson blocked the staging area's overhead light.

"Get back to the team this instant," Stansson ordered the woman. Marria nodded and obediently left Team USA's area.

Gordon glared at Coach Stansson. The two men stared at each other.

"We haven't formally met," said Gordon with

mock politeness. "I'm Gordon Bombay, coach, Team USA."

"I know who you are," said Stansson. Even his voice was flat and lifeless. "I know the competition. I study them. I know their weaknesses."

Then he turned and left.

Gordon grimaced to himself. "Nice meeting you, too," he said, half-aloud.

"WELCOME TEAM USA, COACHED BY GORDON BOMBAY!"

Gordon was startled by the announcement over the loudspeaker. The teams were being introduced.

"It's show time," said Tibbles. "Move it out."

With that, Gordon led Team USA through the doors of the staging area and into the arena. The audience cheered.

After the opening ceremonies ended, the first in the series of showdowns began. Team USA would play Team Trinidad/Tobago, the Islanders.

Team USA scored a series of easy goals against the Islanders. By the middle of the third period it was Team USA 7, Trinidad 1. Team USA knew it had the advantage. After all, how much practice could a team get in a country where the temperature rarely dips below eighty degrees?

Dwayne, Connie, and Ken passed the puck in and around their Trinidadian counterparts with ease. The Trinidad players were tired. They slipped and fell as they tried to keep up. The puck slid toward a Trinidad player, but Ken spun around him and swiped it away. Then Charlie swooped in and shot the puck into the net.

Team USA cheered and high-fived each other.

In the stands behind the Team USA bench sat the kid who had laughed when Portman tried to give him an autograph the day before. He had been watching the game with a cynical smirk on his face. It was clear he didn't think much of Team USA's victory over Trinidad.

"Yo, yo, yo," shouted the kid as the team assembled on the bench. "My little brother could score on those guys."

"Why don't you go bother him, then?" replied Jesse irritably.

The kid sneered. "I ain't even got a brother."

"Jesse," called Gordon. "Quit gabbin' and get out there. Show me you want it."

Jesse slipped on his face guard and skated onto the ice. He would show this kid. He went straight for the puck, then raced toward the net. Just then a Team Trinidad player swooped in from the side and stole the puck. To everyone's surprise, the Trinidad player skated all the way past the blue line and netted an easy goal past Goldberg.

Jesse was furious. He raced over to the player who had stolen the puck from him and pushed him from behind. The player went down. The ref skated over and immediately sent Jesse off the ice. Penalty.

Jesse lumbered over to the penalty box and sat down.

"He dissed you bad!"

Jesse turned. It was that same kid. Jesse made a move to leap toward the kid, but the spectator ambled away through the stands, laughing as he went.

At the other end of the bench, Charlie noticed that Banks had been looking anxiously up toward the stands ever since the game began.

"Don't tell me your dad's here," said Charlie. Charlie knew what winning meant to Banks's father.

"Worse," said Banks without taking his eyes off the stands. "Scouts, man. Look at them."

Charlie looked up. Two men were sitting a few rows up watching the game. They wore dark suits and were scribbling into small notebooks.

Banks skated onto the ice for a line change. He sliced the puck away after it dropped and began maneuvering it toward the goal. But his moves were too fast, too desperate. A Trinidad player stripped the puck from Banks and scored a goal.

Banks skated back to the bench, his eyes darting up at the scouts and their little notebooks.

"Don't worry about the scouts," Charlie told him. "Just play your best—"

But just then Gordon yanked Banks away from the bench.

"What're you doing out there, Banks?" yelled Gordon. "That was embarrassing. I want that goal back. Now! Fulton, Portman, Ken. Line change!"

The three players jumped out on the ice and grooved right into play. Ken got the puck after the drop and chipped it to Fulton, who then passed it to Portman. Fulton followed Portman down the center of the ice, both boys barreling ahead like a couple of bulldozers. The Trinidad line scattered out of their way.

Portman swatted the puck across the front of the net, but the Islanders goalie made a glove save. Portman then took a swat at the goalie's glove with his stick. The glove, with the puck still in it, flew into the net.

The buzzer sounded. The game was over. It was 9–3, Team USA.

The crowd jumped to its feet and cheered.

Team USA took a bow.

10

DOWNTIME

Being the only girls on Team USA, Connie and Julie had become fast friends. That night after the opening games, Connie and Julie were in their dorm room getting ready to turn in. Julie was brushing her hair, and Connie was reading a book.

Julie looked over at Connie. She was so popular, Julie thought. And beautiful. Julie felt so plain next to her.

"It's kind of embarrassing," Julie said as she thought aloud about the last couple of days. "All the attention . . ."

"I love it here," said Connie. "I feel like a movie star or something."

"You're used to it," said Julie. Then she paused. "What's it like to have both Guy and Luis in the palm of your hand?"

"I wish they would *both* just grow up," Connie answered. "American boys can be so immature."

Julie smiled. She knew Connie was referring to Gianni, the handsome boy who was the captain of the Italian team. Before the opening ceremonies earlier that day, Gianni had introduced himself to both girls, but it was obvious that he had special eyes for Connie.

"Mi chiamo Connie," Connie intoned, reading from an Italian phrase book. *"Grazie, prego, Signorina Connie, si, si . . . pasta!"*

Connie looked up at Julie, and both girls giggled knowingly at one another.

"The feather, if you please," requested Goldberg. He, Ken, and Luis were in their dorm room. They were hovering over Dwayne, who was asleep in his bunk.

There was a heaping glob of shaving cream in Dwayne's upturned palm.

Luis pulled the feather from the brim of Dwayne's cowboy hat and passed it ceremoniously to Goldberg. Goldberg began gently tickling Dwayne under the nose with the feather. Dwayne stirred, then sniffled. The boys grinned.

WHAP! Dwayne slapped at his nose and splattered shaving cream all over his face.

Ken, Luis, and Goldberg doubled over with smothered laughter. Amazingly Dwayne didn't wake up! Goldberg began rubbing Dwayne's ear with the feather.

SLAP! This time Dwayne smeared the shaving cream along the side of his face, which was now almost completely covered in foam. The boys couldn't hold back any longer. They broke out in raucous laughter.

Finally Dwayne woke up. "What the—" He pawed at the mess on his face. In retaliation he picked up his pillow and threw it at Goldberg. Goldberg, Ken, and Luis grabbed for their own pillows. They bombarded Dwayne first, but the fight quickly escalated into a free-for-all. Feathers were flying everywhere.

In the next room, Banks was having a hard time falling asleep. All the laughing and screaming coming through the wall wasn't helping. He felt miserable. All he could think about were the talent scouts who had been at the game. All Adam wanted was to play professional hockey. His big break had come today, and instead of impressing the scouts, he had played badly. He had blown it. His life was over.

Banks got out of bed and went into the next room.

"Guys, I need my sleep," he complained. "We've got another game tomorrow."

"It's against Italy," grinned Luis. "No contest. Chill."

"I have to play well," insisted Banks. "The scouts are watching. Please."

Luis, Goldberg, Ken, and Dwayne put down their pillows and looked at each other. They sheepishly turned to go to their beds.

WUMPH! They made a surprise turnabout and attacked Banks with all four pillows. Banks tried to defend himself. It was no use. He was caught in a blizzard of feathers.

Angry at first, Banks soon joined the others in laughter. For the time being, at least, he forgot all about the scouts.

11

A NEW PERSPECTIVE

As Luis had predicted the Italian team was no match for Team USA, which won 11–0. Team USA seemed unbeatable.

Gordon cut short his after-game hang with the kids and retreated to the beach house with Tibbles and Marcy Hendrix. Tibbles had arranged an afternoon reception in Gordon's honor. The house was filled with Hendrix executives, sports journalists, and even some movie stars. After a while Gordon found himself on the patio with Tibbles and Hendrix. They were drinking frothy cappuccinos and breathing in the salty ocean air.

"Bet you didn't know you have so many friends, huh?" Tibbles asked Gordon.

Gordon smiled at Tibbles and Hendrix. "It's nice to be appreciated for your work," he admitted.

"You bet it is," said Hendrix. Then she opened

her briefcase and pulled out a stack of papers. "These are letters of intent that will bind us together should we decide to use you in any and/or all of our product endorsements," she explained to Gordon. "Here you can see the guaranteed fees you will collect. We trust these new numbers are fair."

Gordon glanced at the papers. "Those are nice, fair numbers," he agreed. He couldn't believe how much money they were giving him. "You'll pay me that much just to endorse sports apparel?"

"What do you say?" asked Tibbles.

"Got a pen?" replied Gordon.

Tibbles handed Gordon a pen, and Gordon signed the papers.

"Now there's only one thing left for us to do, Gordon," said Hendrix.

"What's that, Marcy?"

"Enjoy."

Gordon took another sip of his cappuccino. "I can do that," he said smiling.

While Gordon sipped cappuccinos at the elegant beach house, Team USA was finishing up its daily lesson in a classroom on the UCLA campus. Ms. MacKay was just rolling up the map she used for geography as the kids bolted out of the classroom. It was Friday, and she knew the kids were anxious for some fun before their next game on Monday.

Except for Adam Banks. Ms. MacKay had noticed that he didn't seem to be enjoying himself as much as the others.

"Adam," Ms. MacKay called out as Banks headed for the door. "What're you going to do with your free time?"

"Practice," Banks said automatically.

"Practice, practice, practice," said Ms. MacKay. "You're a fourteen-year-old boy in the middle of Los Angeles. Maybe you could try to have a little, oh, I don't know . . . fun?"

"Hockey is fun," said Banks.

"Adam, there's more to life than hockey."

"Not to my life," Banks retorted. "We win here, then I go to the juniors, then the pros. What could be better for a Minnesota boy?"

"What if you don't become a hockey player?" asked Ms. MacKay.

Banks didn't hesitate. "I will," he said.

Ms. MacKay turned to the blackboard and picked up a piece of chalk. "Let's do a little math," she said. "There are how many teams in the National Hockey League?"

"Twenty-four," replied Banks.

Ms. MacKay wrote the number on the blackboard. "How many players on each team?" she asked.

"A team can carry twenty players," answered Banks.

Ms. MacKay wrote that number down as well. Then she began to calculate. "Twenty-four times twenty," she recited as she continued to write. "Four hundred and eighty players. Now, junior hockey leagues nationwide report forty-five thousand members. Let's be generous and say only one third of those are serious about hockey. One third is fifteen thousand players competing for four hundred and eighty slots."

"No," said Banks. "You don't get four hundred and eighty new players every year. Only the top rookies make it into the league."

"That's right," confirmed Ms. MacKay. "So how many rookies make it into the league every year?"

"About fifteen," said Banks.

"Fifteen?" repeated Ms. MacKay. "Fifteen players out of fifteen thousand? That's one in a thousand, Adam. Those aren't very good odds."

Banks stared silently at Ms. MacKay. He felt his heart sink into his stomach. She was right, he realized. The odds were astronomical that he wouldn't make it into the league. What made him think he was good enough, anyway?

"Isn't that the model from the cover of the swimsuit issue?" Gordon asked, pointing as he and Tibbles meandered through the living room of the

Jan and Charlie Conway listen to a Waves hockey game in the back room of Jan and Hans's Sports Shop.

The Waves's Gordon Bombay grimaces in pain after shattering his knee.

Don Tibbles asks Gordon to coach the U.S. hockey team in the
Junior Goodwill Games in Los Angeles.

The reunited Mighty Ducks pose for a team photo with Gordon
and Tibbles.

beach house. Gordon was overwhelmed. He had never seen so many famous people all at once. In person. In *his* house!

Then Gordon did a double take and stopped dead in his tracks. Not three feet from him, chatting with a small group of people, was Pat Riley, the coach of the New York Knicks.

"Go over and introduce yourself," urged Tibbles. "He's a coach. You're a coach. Talk coach stuff."

Gordon was nervous as he approached Coach Riley. Sure, he was coaching Team USA, but Riley was a *real* coach who coached real players, not peewees.

"Excuse me," Gordon stuttered, "Mr.—Pat—I'm Gordon Bombay, coach of Team USA."

"Very nice to meet you," said Riley. "I hear your team is doing very well."

"You have?" squeaked Gordon. He was flattered. "I mean, we *are*. Hey, you haven't done so bad this year yourself."

Just then Terry, Tibbles's young assistant, interrupted to say that Gordon was wanted on the phone. "He says it's urgent," Terry added.

Gordon raced to the dorm, but he couldn't find Banks anywhere. He finally found him in an empty pavilion, shooting pucks against a wall. His suitcases were packed and sitting off to the side. Banks told him about the depressing conversation he had had with Ms. MacKay.

Ten minutes later Gordon tracked down Michele in the classroom. She was seated behind the desk, correcting papers.

"I need to talk to you now!" demanded Gordon angrily.

Michele looked up calmly. "Not in that tone of voice," she said reprovingly.

"Excuse me," insisted Gordon, "but we have to talk."

"You're not my coach, so I suggest better manners."

"You're not my teacher, so quit treating me like a child."

Michele obligingly placed the papers facedown on the desk and waited for Gordon to begin.

"Banks dares to dream of something bigger and you say, No, Adam, dream smaller. My team, all of them, are here because they're special, and all you want to do is tell them how ordinary they are."

"I told Banks the truth, and you know it," Michele said, defending herself.

"The truth is beside the point," argued Gordon.

"He was beating up on himself," explained Michele. "He was miserable. I thought it would give him a better perspective."

"A better perspective?" said Gordon, stunned. "Now my number one scorer doesn't think he stands a chance. You did it on purpose, didn't you?"

Michele shook her head no.

"Yes, you did," insisted Gordon. "You think hockey is just a bunch of guys on skates trying to knock a rubber puck into a net with a long stick!"

"Isn't it?" asked Michele.

"Well, yes. It is," said Gordon. "But it's more than that! You don't know the first thing about sports. You probably don't even sweat."

"I do so sweat!" she snapped. Then she sighed and tried to regain her composure. "Look," she said. "I didn't mean to discourage him."

Gordon looked at her, dumbfounded. "How naive can you be?" he asked her. "My team is different. Your math does not apply to them."

"Now who's being naive," said Michele.

Gordon decided he had heard enough. He wouldn't let a know-nothing schoolteacher ruin *his* team, not to mention ruin his chances of becoming a famous coach.

"You were brought here to teach," he said coldly. "Just do your job."

He left the room and slammed the door behind him. It sent a shudder down Michele's spine.

12

A DAY OFF, AN OFF DAY

Most of Team USA decided to spend their Saturday at Venice Beach.

They were awestruck as they approached the beach from a bicycle path. Los Angeles was such a weird place. It seemed as if people spent all their time in bathing suits. All around them were skateboarders, people playing volleyball, and, out on the waves, surfers.

They were walking along a bike path when they looked up and saw a fleet of Rollerbladers with hockey sticks headed right toward them.

"Jump!" shouted Luis.

They leaped out of the way. The skaters whizzed by without stopping. All except one. It was that kid who had been showing up at the games. The one who had been taunting them since they first arrived.

"Yo, Team USA," he called out. "Hope the hockey isn't interfering with your vacation!" he wisecracked. The kid skated away, laughing.

The players exchanged bewildered glances. Who was this guy? And why was he wherever they went?

The kids found an empty spot on the beach and rolled out their blankets. Connie and Julie worked on their tans.

Ken, Luis, Charlie, and Guy pulled out a flying disk and began throwing it around. There were a few tosses and some acrobatic catches. Then Guy sailed the disk way over Luis's head.

"You did that on purpose," shouted Luis. He knew Guy was still upset because Connie had smiled at him. "You go get it."

"Go get it yourself," retorted Guy.

Ken shook his head wearily and jogged after the disk. He wanted to play, not fight over girls. When he bent down to pick it up, however, he was tackled by eight Vikings. They had been jogging along the beach in their uniforms when they blindsided Ken. One of the Vikings then deliberately smashed his knee into Ken's face. Ken slumped to the ground, his nose dripping with blood.

Charlie, Guy, and Luis ran over to help as soon as they saw the attack. But by then the Vikings had trotted farther down the shore.

"Hey, you stupid jerks!" Charlie shouted after them.

The Vikings kept jogging.

"You better run," warned Luis. "Come back! We'll kick your butts! COWARDS!"

The Vikings did a sudden about-face.

"Uh-oh," said Charlie nervously. "There's more of them than us," he said, "and they're bigger." He did some quick mental calculations. "I say we—"

"RUN!" Ken, Luis, and Guy sprinted off. Charlie brought up the rear, kicking up sand as he went. They did everything they could to lose the Vikings.

The kids darted in and around a maze of sunbathers, dashed under volleyball nets, and jumped over some benches. They raced past a group who were filming a movie on the beach. Nothing could stop them. Nothing . . . except maybe the dead end as they entered a pavilion.

Before they had a chance to correct their mistake, the Vikings players were on them.

"Who's the coward now?" bellowed Olaf, the team captain. The huge Icelandic players moved in on the boys.

"Good question," came a voice from behind them. It was Fulton. Portman was at his side. Now the odds were a little more even.

For a moment it was a stalemate. Nobody moved. Not the Vikings. Not Team USA.

Suddenly the balance of the Vikings team arrived. The Vikings smiled. Team USA cringed.

"What's going on?" asked Coach Stansson.

"They interfered with our workout," complained one of the Vikings.

"They started it!" said Ken angrily. He pulled his sleeve away from his face. "Look at my nose."

"This is between you boys," Stansson said. "I don't want to meddle."

Coach Stansson left the pavilion and continued his jog. It was Team USA 6, Vikings 14. The odds were not good.

Olaf threw the first punch. He hit Fulton squarely in the stomach. Portman jumped on Olaf's back, but two more Vikings pulled him to the ground and pounced on him. Charlie, Ken, Luis, and Guy threw themselves into the mix, but they were quickly overpowered. They were no match for the Vikings.

The fight lasted longer than it should have because the Vikings were enjoying themselves too much.

"What am I going to do with you guys?" asked Gordon. He was escorting his team, most of whom were badly scuffed and bruised, out of police headquarters.

"They were lucky the cops came," said Portman. "We could have handled them."

"Well, you didn't," Gordon reminded Portman. "And now you've given them the mental edge. Therefore, no more beach, no more Beverly Hills. I'm laying down a seven o'clock curfew. So get over to dinner, then straight to the dorms. I want you all to start remembering why you're here. Now get to the bus. Move it."

As the kids scrambled onto the Team USA bus, Charlie straggled behind.

"They jumped us," he said, facing Gordon. "It wasn't fair. Where were you?"

Gordon avoided the question. "I had things to do," he said. He found himself unable to look Charlie in the face.

"Oh, 'things,' " said Charlie sarcastically. "Of course. Sorry. I guess I shouldn't ask."

Gordon stiffened. "I was attending to important team business," he said. His tone was anything but convincing.

"You've been attending to a lot of team business out here," Charlie fired back. "Maybe you should attend more to the team."

"Maybe you should remember that I'm the coach here, Charlie," snapped Gordon. "And that means you do what I say."

Gordon and Charlie glared at each other for a long, thick minute. Finally Charlie turned and climbed onto the bus. Gordon stared at Charlie's back and sighed. We'd been so close once, Gordon thought. Now we're far apart. When did it happen, he wondered. And why?

Gordon couldn't get Charlie out of his mind, and it depressed him. He was supposed to spend Saturday evening with Tibbles and Hendrix. The Hendrix executives had promised him a big night out on the town.

Instead, Gordon went to the gym for a workout. Ever since he dropped the kids off at the dorm, the pain in his knee ached worse than usual. He adjusted a leg-lift machine. Even with the lightest of weights, he could barely bend his knee. The pain was intense.

"I'm sorry for what happened at the beach."

Gordon looked up, startled. It was Marria, Coach Stansson's beautiful assistant.

"Yes," said Gordon. "Me, too. You'd think they'd know better."

"It is Coach Stansson," explained Marria. "He has them, how do you say, so 'pumped up.' They go too far sometimes. I have spoken with him, and he is sorry. Let me make you a peace offering. Do you like ice cream? I'll buy you a double scoop. For détente."

Gordon happily agreed. He welcomed the distraction to get his mind off the mess with Charlie.

And Marria was as beautiful a distraction as he could imagine.

Marria drove Gordon to Westwood, a place where many shops and restaurants stayed open late and they could stroll among the students from the nearby college. Marria made good on her promise and bought ice-cream cones for both of them.

"I thought Iceland was covered with ice," said Gordon as they walked.

"No, it is very green," Marria said, correcting him.

"I thought Greenland was green."

Marria laughed. "Greenland is covered in ice," she said. "Iceland is very nice. I imagine it to be like Minneapolis, where you are from."

"How did you know where I was from?"

"I asked around," Marria answered. "Are you going back home after the Games?"

"I haven't made up my mind," said Gordon. "I've got a lot going on."

"I'm sure you do," Marria said. Then she slipped her arm around his.

They turned the corner and passed a bright, neon-lit music store. They didn't see Fulton and Portman, out on the town, breaking the curfew, come out of the store, carrying shopping bags.

They were dismayed when they spied Gordon

walking arm in arm with a member of the Vikings staff.

"He grounds us for defending ourselves, then he goes out fraternizing with the enemy," growled Portman. "Great coach we got."

They ran back to the dorm to tell the others.

13

ROMANCE, TEAM USA STYLE

Before turning in that night, Guy, Ken, and Averman decided to have a little target practice. They filled up a bucket of water balloons and tossed them out the window. They were trying to hit players from the other teams as they came back to the dorm.

Connie and Julie turned in early that night. They were exhausted from the events of the day and had to rest up for Sunday practice.

Just after they flicked off the light, however, they heard music outside their window.

Connie opened her eyes wide. "Gianni!" she exclaimed, breathlessly. "I knew he'd come!"

Connie excitedly jumped out of bed and ran to the window. The handsome captain of the Italian team was standing in the courtyard below her window, strumming a guitar.

Connie thought back dreamily to the first time she had seen him. It was in the staging area at the coliseum. She was standing next to Julie when Gianni threw her a big smile.

"Haloooo," crooned Gianni, looking up at Connie. "Please . . . what is the name?"

"*Mi chiamo* Connie," she answered in phrasebook Italian.

"No, no," said Gianni, a bit confused.

"Si, si," said Connie, nodding. "I am Connie."

"Not you, signorina," pleaded Gianni. "The other."

Connie was confused. Julie appeared next to her at the window.

"YOU!" Gianni exclaimed gleefully. "Mi amore! What is your name?"

Julie was bewildered. "Julie," she answered tentatively. Gianni responded to Julie's quizzical look by breaking into song. Julie blushed. She was so embarrassed. She also felt bad for Connie.

Connie lowered her head and moved away from the window.

"Hey, Connie," called Julie. "Watch this." She leaned slightly out the window. "Hey, Gianni," she called out. "Please back up into the light. I must see you."

Gianni obeyed willingly. Soon he emerged into the building's bright exterior light.

Julie shouted up to the next floor, "Red alert! Major target below!"

Ken, Guy, and Averman heeded the alert, and within seconds Gianni was being pummeled with water balloons.

Both girls laughed hysterically. They smashed their palms together in a victorious high five. Connie smiled. Julie was a true friend, she realized.

More than that, she was a true teammate.

14

TEAM USA
VERSUS THE VIKINGS

Monday afternoon Team USA was in the locker room preparing for an important game against Team Iceland. Their recent brawl on the beach had shaken their confidence. They weren't certain they could beat them.

The Vikings had shown themselves to be a tightly knit, well-tuned team. And their coach was with them wherever they went. That was more than could be said about Coach Gordon Bombay.

Lately the only time Team USA saw its coach was when he showed up for a game. And even then he was usually late.

Today Gordon showed up on time. He looked different, however. Instead of the relaxed, casual windbreaker and jeans he usually wore to the games, he was dressed in an expensive custom-tailored Italian suit. His hair had been freshly cut and slicked back from his forehead. And he smelled of cologne.

"Nice haircut," commented Averman sarcastically. "What happened? You lose a bet?"

The kids laughed uneasily.

"You have a good time Saturday night, Coach?" asked Fulton. By now everyone knew whom Gordon had been with.

"Not bad," said Gordon, clueless.

Just then another Gordon Bombay popped in through the locker-room door. This wasn't a real, flesh-and-blood Gordon Bombay, however. This was a full-size cardboard cutout of Gordon, complete with a comic-book speech bubble that had him saying, "For my players . . . it's Hendrix or nothing!"

Tibbles smiled proudly at his creation. The kids roared at the sight of the cardboard Gordon.

Next, Tibbles returned carrying a huge trading card that featured a photograph of Team USA. The kids were astonished to see themselves represented larger than life, just like their favorite pro hockey players. Then Tibbles displayed another set of cards. Each one featured an individual player.

"Upper Deck trading cards, Goodwill series," explained Tibbles. "Collect your favorites. They'll be sold in every convenience store around the country."

"Go in for a soda and there you all are," said Gordon excitedly. "Every kid in America will look up to you. 'Hey, I'll trade you a Goldberg for a Fulton!' "

"Every kid in high school will know who you are," added Tibbles. "Winners!"

The kids cheered. They were getting fired up now—fired up to face Team Iceland.

"Let's win this and make it happen!" yelled Gordon. "TEAM USA ALL THE WAY! USA ALL THE WAY!"

"USA ALL THE WAY!" chanted the kids. "USA ALL THE WAY!"

They kept up the chant as they left the locker room and emerged under the bright spotlights of the arena. The crowd cheered as Team USA skated to the bench. Team Iceland had already been introduced and was waiting impatiently for the game to begin.

The players looked across the ice to Team Iceland. The Vikings threw back menacing stares.

Minutes later both teams were on the ice. Portman was on the red line facing off against Gunnar, center for Iceland. They stared each other down waiting for the referee to drop the puck.

"You jumped my teammates, you pay," Portman

said, reminding Gunnar of the recent fight on the beach.

Gunnar sneered and replied in Icelandic. Portman smiled. He couldn't understand a word Gunnar said, but somehow he knew it wasn't a compliment.

Then the puck was dropped. Gunnar moved up for it, but Portman checked him clean, tripping him backward onto the ice. Gunnar lay still. Portman knew it was a fake-out.

A whistle blew shrilly. Portman couldn't believe it.

"I barely touched you," said Portman. "Get up."

But by then the ref had taken Portman by the arm and was escorting him off the ice.

"You took an unprovoked run at him," said the ref.

"Unprovoked?" grunted Portman angrily. "They jumped us at the beach!"

"This ain't no beach," said the ref. "And you're out of the game."

Gunnar slowly raised himself off the ice and skated to his team's bench. Coach Stansson congratulated him as he sat down. Even so, Gunnar frowned. The whole thing had been a fake, and he didn't feel right about it.

The Vikings went on the power play, and within a minute they had scored their first goal. Things went downhill for Team USA from then on. Team

USA just couldn't skate with Team Iceland. By the time the buzzer sounded ending the first period, the Vikings were ahead 4–0.

"We're being blown out!" yelled Gordon as Team USA sat dazed on the bench. "Sloppy play, stupid penalties. You look like a bunch of chickens without heads running around out there!"

"We're doing our best, Coach," Jesse mumbled.

"Your best is not good enough!" Gordon shot back. "Blow this game and we're one loss away from elimination. You guys may want to go home, but I sure don't."

Gordon turned and stormed away.

The kids were dumbfounded. What was Bombay's problem? they asked themselves. Ever since they had arrived in Los Angeles, Gordon seemed different. He was less interested in the team and more interested in himself and his endorsements. He had sold out, they decided. What right did he have to criticize them, anyway? He was never around to coach them. They needed more than their picture on a cereal box to win games.

They felt as if they had been wiped out twice. First by Team Iceland and then by Gordon Bombay.

Meanwhile, Gordon stood sheepishly off to the side. He wouldn't even look at his players. He couldn't. He sensed that they had lost faith in him. His pep talks had degenerated into accusations and put-downs. He felt depressed and dispirited. For the first time he wondered if there really was any hope that they could win.

Dwayne controlled the face-off against Gunnar at the start of the second period. He shouted rodeo-style whoops and yells as he scooted the puck across the ice. Then two Iceland defensemen rammed him into the boards, stole the puck easily, and skated toward the net. Dwayne crumpled to the ice like a rag doll.

On the bench Gordon blew out his cheeks and turned to Ken.

"Ken, what can you do for me?" he asked, sounding desperate.

"Triple aerial with a Hamill Camel should split the defense," said Ken. "Then a pirouetting half toe-touch for the goal."

"Show it to me, son!" said Gordon as he pushed Ken out onto the ice.

A minute later Ken skated back to the bench, doubled over, the wind knocked out of him. The Vikings had demolished him.

Meanwhile, Banks managed to get hold of the puck and skated down the ice. Luis sped ahead, ready to take the pass. His path was suddenly blocked, however, by a Viking who tripped him and sent him crashing into the boards.

Team Iceland passed the puck easily among themselves. They moved confidently and gracefully. One Viking took the puck straight to Goldberg at the net. Goldberg committed himself, and just then the Viking flicked the puck to a fellow winger. Goldberg was completely off balance. The second winger effortlessly sent the puck deep into the net.

Gordon turned to the bench. "Fulton," he called. "Go out and blast one."

Fulton jumped out onto the ice and waited for the puck. He got a pass from Banks, wound up, and slammed it. It whistled through the air like a bullet, scattering Team Iceland players out of its path.

But the Team Iceland goalie stood his ground. His glove hand went up. WHACK! The puck slammed against leather.

Fulton was stunned.

He *caught* the puck?

Team USA was incredulous. Their secret weapon had just taken his best shot and come up zeroes. Fulton slumped his shoulders. He skated slowly off the ice.

Nothing had changed by the middle of the third period. Team Iceland was demolishing Team USA. The once-mighty Ducks were losing, *badly.*

From the bench Banks looked around nervously. He saw the scouts put their notepads away and get up to leave.

Banks put himself on the ice. Immediately he

hustled to scoop up a loose puck, evaded two defenders, and frantically made his way toward the goal. The fans cheered. The scouts stopped and turned.

Banks was a one-man hockey team zooming across the ice. A defenseman skated to intercept him. Banks let him close, jerked left, then swerved right around him. Fake-out. He was too fast. He slipped by another defender and skated straight on goal. He shot. SCORE!

The fans roared. Gordon and the team cheered. The scouts pulled out their notebooks again and began scribbling.

Suddenly Banks doubled over with pain. Out of nowhere a stick had come down on his wrist like a tomahawk. Another whistle. Banks crumpled to the ice and grabbed his wrist. The Team Iceland player who had hacked him grinned maliciously as the ref pulled him off the ice.

Gordon was beside himself. It was one of the most blatant cheap shots he had ever seen.

Then the buzzer sounded. Game over. It was Vikings 12, Team USA 1.

15

GORDON REMEMBERS GORDON

"Ms. Hendrix is very, uh, disappointed," said Tibbles diplomatically as he cornered Gordon outside the locker room. Marcy Hendrix was a bit more blunt in her appraisal.

"I'm furious!" she roared. "Bombay, did you think Hendrix was interested in backing losers? I was told you were a contender!"

"We just didn't have the magic tonight," Gordon lied.

"Well, *get* the magic," she ordered him sternly. "And get it fast. Because if you don't, you'll be back in Palookaville shoveling snow for the city. And you won't work in hockey again, anywhere, ever. I can assure you of that."

Hendrix turned and marched away, her footsteps echoing down the hall.

"Gordon," began Tibbles nervously. He was

clearly rattled. "You represent a large investment for Hendrix. If you don't turn the team around, you will be a very *bad* large investment. Please," he pleaded, "for both our sakes, don't let that happen."

Gordon didn't know what to say. He had let Tibbles and Hendrix Apparel down. If he let them down again, he'd be out of a job. He wasn't going to let that happen.

There was only one thing to do: work harder. That meant no more Mr. Nice Guy to his players. He had babied them too much already.

The Team USA players were still sulking in the locker room when Gordon entered. They hadn't even bothered to change out of uniform. They looked depressed and dejected.

"That was pathetic!" Gordon shouted. "You were brought here to play hockey."

"What about you?" demanded Jesse.

"What about me?" snapped Gordon.

"*Their* coach knew everything about us," said Julie. "They were ready for us."

"You're spendin' all your time drivin' convertibles, talkin' to those sponsor fools," added Luis.

"Or hanging out with that Iceland lady," Fulton said. Gordon shot him a look. "We saw you two Saturday night," Fulton added.

"What I do doesn't matter!" shouted Gordon.

He read them the riot act, and when the players groaned and complained, he told them he didn't care whether they liked the new rules or not.

That evening after dinner Gordon ordered the team to the practice rink. He started them at the beginning, working them in everything from basic skating to breakaways. When they were done with the drills, he started them over again.

The next morning the exhausted players were awakened by the shrill sound of Gordon's whistle. After breakfast they were marched into the weight room.

Gordon worked them hard. Goldberg and Luis were on the treadmills. Portman and Fulton were lifting barbells. Averman was doing chin-ups. Connie was doing step aerobics; Dwayne and Ken struggled in vain to keep up with her. Charlie worked a pull-down bar. Julie was doing stretches on a mat.

Banks was doing leg presses. It was the only exercise machine he could use without taxing his injured wrist. He couldn't let anyone know just how much pain he was really in.

The rest of the day was more of the same. The kids were being worn ragged.

The next morning Ms. MacKay burst cheerfully into the classroom and opened her lesson-plan book. She noticed immediately that the kids were anything but eager to begin. Several students had their faces buried in their arms on their desks. The others could barely keep their eyes open.

They were exhausted.

Gordon was in the team locker room waiting for the kids when Michele walked in. He looked impatient and angry.

"Ms. MacKay," said Gordon, surprised. "Where are my kids?"

"It's my job to see to the children's health and welfare," she said in a businesslike tone. "I made the determination that they needed a day off."

"You can't do that!" said Gordon.

Michele explained in no uncertain terms that she *could* do that. "You're running those children ragged," she said. "They call you Captain Blood."

"I'm preparing them for battle," explained Gordon. "You don't have any idea what it takes to—"

"Save it," Michele cut in. "It's a game, Gordon. You said it yourself. Games should be fun."

"That was before," Gordon said, suddenly serious. "The stakes are a little higher now."

"Really? For whom?"

"For everyone. We win, we can go on to bigger things."

"The kids are all going home after this, win or lose," said Michele. "Gold medals or not. They're going to go back to high school, pimples, puberty, the whole thing. The stakes are higher for *you,* Gordon. And they shouldn't be playing to get your face on a box of USA Crunch."

Gordon was stunned into silence.

She was right.

Before returning to the beach house, Gordon stopped off at Venice Beach and laced up into his Rollerblades. He hadn't been on a pair of skates since his knee injury.

His first strides were weak and uncertain. But soon he noticed that his knee wasn't hurting as much anymore. His skating became stronger with each stride. He felt like a kid again.

Gordon picked up his hockey stick and threw a street puck to the ground. He guided the puck down the sidewalk, pushing it from side to side with the stick. Then he brought the blade back and took a full slap shot. The puck went flying through the air and into a trash can.

SCORE!

Gordon felt the same way he had all those years ago when his father used to watch him practice on the pond back home. He remembered how much he had enjoyed playing the game back then—how much *fun* it used to be.

When he arrived at the beach house he noticed that all the lights were out. Gordon stopped in the hallway. "Tibbles?" he called out.

"This is no place for a coach," came a familiar but unexpected voice.

Gordon was startled. He flicked on the light. Jan was sitting in a chair, staring out to sea.

"Jan," said Gordon. "What are you doing here?"

"I thought you might like some hasenpfeffer," he said, turning to Gordon and smiling.

Gordon smiled, too. He put down his gear and sat in a chair next to Jan. "It's good to see you," he said. "Who's watching the shop?"

"We're closed," answered Jan. "First time in ten years. I watched the Iceland game on television. Who was that guy in the suit with the wet hair? Was it raining?"

Gordon sighed and shook his head. "You came two thousand miles to make fun of me?" he said. "You could have done that on the phone."

"No," said Jan. "I came to see you as a friend. On TV I saw a man who seemed like he needed one."

Gordon looked away from Jan, toward the beach. "I don't know what I need," he said softly. "Things are really different out here. All of a sudden I'm wearing nice clothes and people are smiling at me. I'm talking to Pat Riley at a party where the bartenders are actors and the actors want to be directors. Everybody wants to be somebody else, and nobody eats red meat."

"Everything is different out here, yes, Gordon,"

said Jan. "Everything except *you*. You are still Gordon Bombay."

Gordon laughed. "Who's that?" he asked with a smirk.

"A coach. A friend. Someone the kids look up to and love."

Jan got up from his chair and went into the kitchen. A minute later he returned with two bowls of hot food. Gordon smiled.

"Hasenpfeffer?" asked Gordon.

"Chef Boyardee," answered Jan.

Both men laughed as they plunged into their dinner.

16

THAT BELMONT KID

Game day. Normally Gordon would have his players rest up before a match, but today he had a surprise for them.

"I can't believe Captain Blood is going to make us train on game day," groaned Connie. She and the rest of the team were assembled at a running track, waiting for Gordon to arrive.

"Hey, yo! Team USA!" a voice called to them. The kids looked over to the side of the track. It was that kid again, the one who had been following them ever since they arrived in Los Angeles. He was wearing Rollerblades and gear.

"What're you gonna do today? A million jumping jacks?"

Then he burst out laughing.

"I'm getting pretty sick of you," shouted Jesse.

"I'm getting sick of seeing the USA represented by a bunch of whinin' babies," the kid snapped back.

Jesse stiffened. "Too bad you can't back up that mouth," he said tauntingly.

"Me and my boys could take you anytime, anywhere," the kid shot back.

"I don't see no boys," smirked Jesse.

"I got 'em waiting. Grab your gear, and let's go play some schoolyard puck. Or maybe you forgot what it's like to play for pride."

Jesse was wired for the challenge. But Banks held him back. "We got a game tonight," said Banks. "Coach might—"

"Might what?" snarled the kid. "Get mad at you and make you run laps? Look at you now."

The players exchanged embarrassed glances. The kid was annoying, their faces seemed to say, but he was right.

Jesse nodded. "Let's do it."

When Gordon and Jan arrived at the track ten minutes later, there was no sign of Team USA.

"Looking for your team?"

Gordon and Jan turned simultaneously. Marria had just pulled up to the track in a convertible.

"Have you seen them?" asked Gordon, clearly worried.

"I have, yes," answered Marria. "They boarded a bus to play hockey at Belmont High School. That is where they went."

"We have a game in a few hours!" complained Gordon incredulously. "I don't want them playing pickup."

"Hop in," offered Marria. "I will take you to them."

"You know where Belmont is?" asked Jan suspiciously.

"No, but I have a map. How far can it be?"

Gordon looked at Jan, gave him a what-else-can-we-do look, and climbed into the convertible. Reluctantly Jan got in, too.

There was something about Marria that Jan didn't trust. As they pulled out of the parking lot, he sat back and hoped that he was wrong.

Team USA stood in the school yard facing their opponents: a group of seven black and Latino boys in Rollerblades and with sticks. Instead of professional knee guards, however, the Belmont kids had tied magazines around their legs. And instead of hockey masks, they wore modified football helmets.

"Yo, thanks for comin' out," said James, the leader of the Belmont kids. "Russ has been tellin' me you guys are chokin' big time. Thought we'd try to help you out."

"*You're* gonna help *us?*" said Luis, laughing. "How?"

"We know you can talk to the press and sign autographs," said Russ. He was just finishing tying some newspapers around his shins. "We'll show you something you might have forgot."

"Like how to play like Team USA," said another boy, Hector.

"What would *you* know about it?" snarled Portman.

He got his answer a short time later when James pummeled him into the fence and stole the puck. Portman bounced off the fence and vainly tried to retrieve the puck, but James roughly checked him again.

"You gotta earn every inch," James told Portman. "And when you get mad, you gotta keep it to yourself . . . until the time is right."

Team USA tried to gain control of the puck. They used all their best drilling techniques, including the triple deke. But they were no match for this streetwise grunge team.

The Belmont kids seemed to know where the puck was going before it even got there. They glided across the hard blacktop like well-choreographed dancers. They even communicated plays to each other in their own special code.

Most important, they were having fun.

By comparison, Team USA seemed flat-footed. They were out of sync on every play. Jesse stole the puck and passed it to Luis. Luis zipped around two defenders and took a shot. It went wide of the trash-can goal.

James hustled in and retrieved the puck so fast that no Team USA player could catch him. He zoomed toward the goal and flicked in an easy score.

Russ noticed that Banks hovered on the periphery and had a weak grip on his stick.

"You too good for us?" Russ asked Banks.

"Nah," replied Banks. "Got a bad wrist. Can't hold the stick with two hands."

"Then don't," said Russ. "Just use the one till the other gets better."

Russ grabbed his own stick with one hand and showed Banks what he meant. Banks tried it and was surprised that he could deke with one hand. He was amazed. Grinning from ear to ear, Banks forgot about his bad wrist and jumped headfirst into the game.

Meanwhile, Russ had tapped his stick on the ground and was calling for a pass. Hector sent him the puck. Russ leaned over and set the puck on its side. The players stopped and watched.

Russ took his shot. The puck wobbled clumsily toward the goal. It looked laughable until it landed and scooted past Goldberg into the net.

Goldberg shook his head and threw down his stick in frustration.

"What kind of shot was that?" asked Fulton, totally amazed.

"That's my knucklepuck," explained Russ. "Hard to be accurate, but it drives the goalies crazy."

After a while, Team USA finally began to get into the swing of things. The Belmont kids played freely, energetically, and without inhibition. That feeling began to rub off on the Team USA players. They soon found themselves dancing around the court and laughing.

By the end of the game, Team USA felt less like a Hendrix franchise and more like who they really were: a group of *friends* having fun playing hockey.

"It's getting late," said Russ finally. "You guys better get goin' back."

"Thanks for the tips," said Charlie. "Really."

"Who won?" asked Luis.

"Who knows, man," said James. "You played solid. Hard. Now take that and kick those Viking butts all the way back to Iceland!"

17

COACH MACKAY

Jan wasn't wrong. After what seemed like hours of driving through a completely unfamiliar city, Marria finally pulled into the parking lot of Belmont High. Gordon and Jan jumped out.

"Let me go check around the side," said Gordon. He disappeared around the corner of the school.

"Jan, maybe you should go look on the other side," suggested Marria. He gave her a suspicious glance. "I'll wait here," she promised.

Jan nodded reluctantly.

But Team USA was nowhere to be seen. Nor, for that matter, was Marria when Gordon and Jan reappeared in front of the school yard. They were stranded.

Gordon cursed himself. He had been set up. That much was obvious. Game time was less than an hour away. Team USA was already demoralized. Without a coach they'd be . . . sitting ducks.

Gordon and Jan started walking. They had to get to the rink, but they had a problem. They had no idea where it was.

Team USA sat on the bench nervously waiting for their coach to show. "The Star-Spangled Banner" had been sung. Their opponent, Team Germany, was about to take the ice.

The ref skated over to the bench.

"I'm sorry," he said. "Without a coach behind the bench, you can't play. That's all there is to it."

"No," argued Charlie. "You can't do that. We have a coach."

"Where?"

"There!" said Charlie, pointing. The kids turned and glared.

"Ms. MacKay!" shouted Charlie. "I mean . . . Coach! Coach MacKay!"

Charlie led the confused Ms. MacKay to the bench.

"Charlie, what are you doing?" she asked.

"Pretend you're our coach or we forfeit the game," begged Charlie.

"I don't know anything about coaching," replied Ms. MacKay.

"Pretend or we're out of the tournament," insisted Charlie. He duckwalked her up to the ref. "Here she is," Charlie said. "Here's our coach." Ms.

MacKay gave the ref a timid smile. He appeared unconvinced. She looked apprehensively at the kids, then at the crowd filing into the arena. She was a nervous wreck. It's now or never, she told herself, screwing up her courage.

"What are you waiting for?" she snapped at the ref finally. "The ice to freeze? Let's play!"

The kids cheered as the ref turned and skated back to center ice.

It was game time.

Gordon and Jan waited at a bus stop. They had been waiting an awfully long time, and Gordon was pacing furiously back and forth. A car came down the street. Gordon ran over to the curb and held out his thumb, but the car zoomed by.

"Thanks a lot, buddy!" shouted Gordon. "You just let your country down!"

Gordon looked at his watch. His shoulders dropped. It was game time. He walked dejectedly back to the bench.

"That's it," Gordon said to Jan. "The game's started. I've blown it. I'm not there for them."

"No," agreed Jan. "But you tried to be."

"It doesn't matter," said Gordon. "I guess I didn't try hard enough. Jan, they're all I've got."

Jan put his arm around Gordon's shoulder. "It's not over," he whispered.

Just then their brooding was interrupted by the

blaring of a car stereo. They looked up. A car was cruising slowly down the street. The kids inside the car were staring straight at Gordon and Jan.

"Maybe they will give us a ride," said Jan, rising.

"Easy, Jan," Gordon said nervously, holding him back. "We might have some trouble here."

Jan stood up. "No trouble," he scoffed. "You're the coach of Team USA. People should want to help us."

"Jan, don't," insisted Gordon, but it was too late. Jan had already approached the car and was tapping on its window. The window came down.

It was Russ and the Belmont kids.

"I thought it was you, Coach Bombay," Russ called out. "What're you doin' out here?"

"See?" Jan turned to Gordon. "They know you."

"This is kind of a bad neighborhood," said another kid from the backseat.

Gordon joined Jan at the car. "Can you help us?" he pleaded.

The door flew open instantly. Jan and Gordon climbed in.

"Hit it!" Jan commanded.

Russ laughed as the car roared off down the street.

Amazingly enough, Team USA was holding its own against Germany. Ms. MacKay sat anxiously on the bench, where Averman was busy instructing her in the fine points of coaching.

"Go—skate—that's the way!" Averman said patiently, feeding her her lines.

Ms. MacKay jumped up. "GO! SKATE! THAT'S THE WAY!" she shouted to the players on the ice.

"Say 'line change,' " Averman whispered to her.

"Line change," Ms. MacKay requested primly, and sat down.

"Shout it," Averman suggested.

Ms. MacKay stood up again. "LINE CHANGE!" she called out.

Five players instantly came skating off the ice as five substitutes noisily vaulted the boards.

Ms. MacKay broke into a huge grin. She never knew she could do that.

Later, Ms. MacKay was shocked when Luis was sent sprawling onto the ice.

"That guy tripped Luis," she complained to Averman. "Isn't that bad?"

"It's horrible," Averman agreed. "Let the ref know how you feel."

Ms. MacKay nodded and strode over to the ref. "Luis Mendoza was tripped," she said indignantly. "That was unfair. There should be a punishment."

"Penalty," suggested Averman mildly.

The ref obliged by blowing his whistle. The German player was pulled off the ice.

Averman threw Ms. MacKay a thumbs-up. She smiled and wiped her forehead. She had actually broken a sweat.

Team USA had a power play.

Outside the rink, Gordon jumped out of the car and raced into the arena. Jan, Russ, and the Belmont kids followed as Gordon descended through the stands and reached the Team USA bench.

"I'm here," Gordon announced. "How're we doing?"

"Where have you been?" demanded Michele.

"I'll explain later," answered Gordon. "Right now I want to coach the team. Please."

Instantly Michele had noticed something different in Gordon's voice. She wasn't certain what it was, but she liked what she heard. "Be my guest. They're all yours." They both smiled.

Gordon huddled around the kids on the bench.

"I'm back," Gordon explained. "I'm back and ready to coach. For real this time."

The players weren't about to be fooled so easily.

"We don't need you to coach us," said Portman. "We're doing fine."

There was an awkward moment of silence. Then Charlie stepped forward. "Coach," he said, throwing a quick backward glance at his teammates. "We don't want you to coach Team USA anymore."

Gordon lowered his head. He couldn't blame them. He had acted selfishly, thinking only of his own benefit and not of the team. "We want you to coach the Ducks!" Charlie said.

Gordon looked up into Charlie's face. He was smiling. Then he looked at the rest of the kids. They were smiling at him, too.

The score was tied 2–2 when the whistle blew. The third period was drawing to a close. There were only twenty seconds left in the game.

QUACK!

Heads turned curiously in the stands, trying to locate the source of the strange sound.

QUACK! QUACK!

The arena grew silent as all eyes fell on the coach of Team USA.

He had a duck decoy in his mouth!

"Quack," muttered Charlie on the bench.

"Quack, quack," added Averman, a little louder.

"Quack, quack, quack!" Even Portman joined in on the chant.

Soon Team USA was quacking together in one huge victory cheer.

The puck was dropped to resume play, but a German winger slapped it into the stands. The ref blew the whistle. Less than fifteen seconds to play.

Gordon gathered his team around him.

"We're gonna be Ducks now," he began, "and Ducks fly together!"

"All right!" cheered Jesse.

"Where do we come from?" asked Gordon.

"The pond!" shouted Charlie, Averman, Gold-berg, Fulton, Guy, Connie, and Banks.

"What do Ducks do?" Gordon asked.

"Fly together!" they answered in unison.

"Old Ducks, show the new Ducks," Gordon said. "The Flying V! NOW!"

The players from the old Ducks team flocked onto the ice. Jesse controlled the puck, and the team immediately assumed the V formation. Jesse guided the puck from behind the team as the wedge moved down the ice. The Flying V repelled German players as they went. At the last second Jesse flipped the puck to Banks, who knocked it into the net with a one-handed stab.

The audience roared as the scoreboard lit up. The game was over. Winner: Team USA!

In the stands Coach Stansson and Marria looked on with dismay. Their plan to keep Gordon away from his team had failed. Without this win Team USA would have been out of the tournament.

"They should not have advanced," growled Stansson.

"Stupid Duck nonsense," said Marria bitterly. "If we play them again, we'll destroy them."

"We certainly will," said Stansson as he led Marria out of the arena.

18

EVERYONE'S A DUCK

In the locker room after the game, Team USA—
the Ducks—high-fived each other. They felt hope-
ful again. Victory was in the air.

Everyone congratulated Banks on scoring the
goal. They felt exhilarated. But the only thing
Banks could feel was the stabbing pain in his
wrist. He sat at his locker and began rewrapping
his wrist in sports tape.

"Nice game tonight, Adam," said Gordon, coming up behind him. Banks twisted around, startled. He quickly lowered his bandaged wrist,
trying to hide it from his coach.

"Imagine how you'd do with two good wrists,"
said Gordon.

"It's fine, Coach," insisted Banks. "Just a little
sore."

"I should have spotted this right away," said Gordon. "I wasn't doing my job."

"I'm fine, Coach," Banks insisted again. "Really. I can play tomorrow. I swear."

Gordon held out his hockey stick and told Banks to rotate it with his injured hand. Banks grimaced in pain. Gordon shook his head.

"I have to bench you, Adam," he said. "You could injure yourself permanently."

Banks began to panic. "No," he cried. "Coach, I gotta play. The scouts are all here watching me. This is my shot."

"Adam," said Gordon. "You're young. You're going to have a lot of shots. Believe me."

Banks was nearly in tears. "But, Coach," he pleaded. "My dad is counting on me."

Gordon sat down next to Banks. "My dad worked a lot when I was a kid," he said. "So when he made it to a game, believe me, I wanted to score a hundred goals for him. He was proud of me because I was his son and I tried my best. I know your dad feels the same way."

Banks sighed and slowly nodded his head.

"Come on," said Gordon. "Let's go get that hand X-rayed."

"Okay," said Banks. "But I'm comin' back the second it's better."

"Darn right you are," agreed Gordon. "We need you."

That evening Gordon moved out of the beach house and into the dorm so he could be closer to his players. He knew he had to win back their confidence. He had to show them that he would be there for them, whenever, wherever.

At practice the next day the players smiled appreciatively when Gordon walked into the rink wearing his familiar old bomber jacket and chinos. He was carrying the full-size Bombay-Hendrix cardboard cutout, the trading cards, and the USA Crunch cereal box with Team USA's picture on it. He walked out to center ice and dumped it all into a trash barrel.

To the kids' nodding approval, he lit a match and dropped it in. The promotional props burst into flames.

In chorus Team USA tapped their sticks against the ice to show their approval.

"New attitude means new players," announced Gordon. Then he blew the duck call. A door opened and Russ emerged, suited up in a Team USA uniform.

"With Banks out we have a roster spot open," explained Gordon. "Any objections?"

The kids nodded in acceptance of Russ.

"Thanks," said Russ. He wobbled unsteadily onto the ice. "But I'm not too good on these ice skates."

"That's all right," said Gordon. "I got you a private tutor." He turned toward the bench. "Hey, Banks! Over here."

"Me?" Banks walked over from the sidelines.

"Yeah," said Gordon. "You just got a bad wing. You can still skate, can't you? Teach him to fly."

Banks looked at Russ, then smiled. "Yeah," he said, nodding. "Okay."

"All right," said Gordon. "We're coming together, Ducks." Gordon could feel the change in his team already. "Jan is here for us. The magic is back; I feel it. We just need one more thing."

Once again Gordon blew the duck call. It was aimed at someone standing behind the team. They turned. It was Ms. MacKay.

"We want you to be our assistant coach," Gordon told her. The Ducks enthusiastically tapped their sticks and cheered.

"I don't know anything about hockey," she said, blushing.

"We consider that a plus." Gordon smiled. "Give it a try."

Gordon held out the duck decoy. Ms. MacKay shyly took it and put it to her lips. She took a deep breath and blew. The blast echoed throughout the stadium.

It was drill time.

First, Gordon led the team around the rink commando style—on their stomachs—with himself in the lead.

Meanwhile, Jan was working with Luis. He set up a row of soda cans as an obstacle course. Luis skated in and out, trying not to overturn the cans.

Jan did a lot of restacking of soda cans that morning. After a while, however, Luis was skating better. Jan smiled and patted Luis on the back.

The team drilled hard on their breakaways, passes, slap shots, and dekes. With each routine the kids got a bit better, smoother. Gordon couldn't help but notice that they seemed more confident and self-assured. Watching his players drill, Gordon felt something he hadn't felt in a long time: pride.

Later Gordon noticed Tibbles sitting alone in the stands. He skated over.

"Hendrix fired me," Tibbles told Gordon. He shook his head slowly. "Can you believe it?" He tried to smile. "I just came to say good-bye. And good luck. Sorry to put you through everything, but at least you still have your Ducks." He stood up to leave. "I'll see ya', Gordo."

"Wait, Don," said Gordon. "I could always use one more in the flock. Let me hear you quack."

"Quack?" Tibbles asked, confused. Gordon gave him a mischievous smirk.

A little while later, a terrified Don Tibbles was on the ice, suited up in goalie pads in front of the net. One by one the Ducks gleefully took their positions at the blue line.

"Ready?" Gordon asked his team.

"QUAAAACK!" Tibbles screamed as he was pummeled with a shower of pucks. The kids burst into laugher. Even Tibbles joined in.

Later, when the kids hit the showers, Gordon sat by himself on the bench. There were only two more days before the two top teams would be competing for the championship. Only two more days to get his team in top shape. He shook his head, cursing himself for neglecting them these past weeks.

Would two days be enough time?

19

DUCK PLAYS

USA BLANKS AUSTRIA, 4–0! screamed the newspaper headline.

Playing flawless hockey, Team USA had won a crucial game and now was only one win away from going head-to-head with the Vikings. The old Ducks magic was back, Gordon thought. But would it last?

After the game with Team Austria, Gordon and his players gathered in the locker room to watch a videotape of the Vikings' last game. Charlie stopped the tape after each play while Gordon diagrammed it on a blackboard.

By the end of their session they understood the Vikings' strategy inside and out.

The next day, as Team USA was suiting up for a critical game against Team Russia, the locker-room door opened, and Gordon walked in with a surprise guest.

A hush fell instantly over the locker room as the kids recognized who it was: Wayne Gretzky.

"The Great One!" Charlie shouted excitedly. The team noisily huddled around Gretzky, yelling and cheering.

"You guys aren't so bad yourselves," said Gretzky, returning their compliments. "Now that Canada is out, I just wanted to say Go, Ducks."

"Can you sign my stick, Great One," asked Banks, awestruck. "I mean, Wayne . . . sir . . . *Mr.* Great One?"

"Sure, Banks," said Gretzky. He signed Adam's stick on the blade.

Banks was taken aback. "You know who I am?" he asked.

Gretzky gave him a "duh" look and pointed to his name stitched onto the back of his jersey. Banks blushed red with embarrassment, but everyone laughed.

Thirty minutes later, Team USA took the ice against Team Russia. By the middle of the third period of this tightly contested match the teams were deadlocked 3–3. It was about then that a Russian player missed a slap shot and accidentally high-sticked Averman, who went down hard against the boards. Penalty. Power play to Team USA.

Deciding it was time to introduce their new secret weapon, Gordon sent Russ out onto the ice. After controlling the puck, Dwayne flipped it to Jesse, who passed it to Russ inside the blue line. Russ wound up and let loose with the knuckle-puck. The puck skipped off the ice and wobbled in a looping arc toward the net. The Russian goalie made a grab for the puck, but at the last second it dropped like a brick and skipped into the net.

SCORE!

Then the buzzer rang, ending the game. Team USA 4, Team Russia 3.

The audience went wild.

Gordon and Michele hopped up and down and hugged each other. It was pure pandemonium. The arena was rocking from fans stomping their feet. Everywhere people were waving flags and cheering, "Go, USA! Go, USA!"

The stands were a sea of happy, smiling faces, except for two notable exceptions: Wolf Stansson and Marria.

Neither one was in the mood to celebrate. At least, not yet.

20

COACH VERSUS COACH

The mood of the team on the night before game day was tense. The next day Team USA would face off against Team Iceland in the championship game of the Junior Goodwill Games. By then it would all be over.

Gordon instructed his players to show up at the rink that evening for practice. But not in uniform, he told them. "In your street clothes," he said. The kids were confused.

"Shouldn't we be in our hockey gear?" Luis asked Gordon later when the team had assembled at the rink.

"It will be our last practice," replied Gordon. "And that means—"

"The return of Captain Blood?" suggested Averman.

"Nope," said Gordon, smiling. "It means let's have some *fun.*"

Gordon kicked a huge beach ball out onto the ice. The kids charged after it. They slipped and slid, trying to get control of it.

Meanwhile, Gordon helped Michele lace on a pair of skates. It was her first time on skates, and Gordon guided her slowly across the ice, then let go. She skated unsteadily, lost her balance, and suddenly began to fall backward.

Gordon rushed up and caught her before she hit the ice.

"Nice catch," she said. Gordon smiled. Just then the beach ball bounced off Gordon's head, and he playfully pantomimed that he was falling.

Everyone was having fun, even Tibbles. He was a terrible skater and couldn't control his direction. He'd keep falling, laugh, and try again.

The players had organized a game of ice soccer with the beach ball. At one point, however, Julie kicked the ball too hard. It flew into the stands, and when a couple of kids went after it they bumped into Wolf Stansson. He had the ball clamped between his hands. Marria stood beside him, and behind her were the Team Iceland players.

"Playtime is over," growled Stansson. "We have the ice now."

With a loud POP! Stansson crushed the ball between his huge hands.

Gordon skated over. "We have the ice," Stansson said. "You and your little rink rats must leave."

"The only thing little was your career in the pros," sneered Gordon.

Stansson returned Gordon's stare, and his expression became even more stern. "At least I *had* a shot," he said, taunting Gordon. "I was there."

"You were a disgrace," concluded Gordon. He turned to address Marria. "Hey, Mata Hari, I never thanked you for the ride."

"My pleasure," Marria said nastily.

"Not for long," Gordon promised. He turned to his team. "Come on, Ducks. We're through here."

The players hesitated.

"I said off the ice," Gordon insisted.

Reluctantly the players began skating off toward the runway.

"You can still move on the ice?" called out Stansson to Gordon. "Well, please, play a little with me. Show me you're not the failure everyone says you are. Show me that famous triple deke your dear daddy taught you. Or was it your mommy?"

Gordon froze, then turned. His mouth was set in a hard, thin line. Stansson reached behind a bench and produced two sticks and a puck. He tossed one of the sticks to Gordon.

Jan moved up behind Gordon. "Gordon, no," he warned. "Your knee isn't strong enough."

Gordon ignored Jan's warning. "Three bar," he told Stansson. "First one to hit both posts and the crossbar. Got to take it out past the blue line."

"I know the game," said Stansson. "In Iceland it's called—"

"I didn't ask," said Gordon curtly.

Gordon skated out onto the ice and waited for Stansson behind the blue line. The puck was at his feet. Stansson skated out to meet him. Suddenly Stansson stole the puck! His quick move took Gordon by surprise. DING! Stansson smashed the puck against the right post.

The Vikings cheered.

Gordon retrieved the puck after it ricocheted off the goalpost and skated in a wide arc across the ice. Stansson trailed after him, stabbing at the puck with his stick. Gordon faked as if to lose the puck, and Stansson lunged for it. Just then Gordon pushed the puck around Stansson and slapped it against the left post. CLANG!

Now it was the Ducks turn to cheer. It was 1–1.

Gordon and Stansson met each other at the blue line. The puck lay between them. Stansson suddenly swiped at it, missed, and Gordon came away with it. Furious, Stansson leaned in and elbowed

Gordon hard in the stomach. Gordon crumpled onto the ice.

Smiling to himself, Stansson stole the puck and prepared to shoot. Suddenly Stansson's stick went flying out of his hands. Gordon had come charging up behind Stansson like a stampeding buffalo. As Stansson cursed Gordon in Icelandic, Gordon hustled to retrieve the puck. With a smooth flick of the wrist, Gordon knocked the puck into the right post.

The Ducks exploded in cheers.

Stansson was livid with rage. Never had he been so humiliated.

"Bad news," Gordon explained to him matter-of-factly. "That wasn't even my triple deke."

Stansson angrily picked up his stick.

Gordon nonchalantly guided the puck behind the blue line and prepared for his next move. Stansson skated in front of him like a panther silently contemplating its next kill.

"One more and it's over," Gordon reminded him politely. "Oh, and by the way, you owe me a beach ball."

Gordon grinned and slowly moved in on the puck. Stansson had his eyes glued to Gordon's every move. He knew what was coming. He smiled meanly as Gordon pulled in the puck in preparation for his famous triple deke.

ONE! Gordon deked left.

TWO! He deked right.

THREE!

"No!" yelled the Ducks as Stansson deliberately slashed Gordon in the knee.

Gordon screamed in pain and collapsed in a heap onto the ice. It was as if a hammer had come down on his bad knee. Jan and Ms. MacKay ran out to him on the ice.

Meanwhile, the Ducks had moved in on the Vikings. They were ready for a fight.

"No, Ducks!" Gordon called out, seeing what was happening. "Hold it! We're better than they are. We know it."

The Ducks stopped. Gordon was right.

Jan and Michele helped lift Gordon to his feet. He struggled to stand up on his good leg, then waved them off as he stood on both legs.

"Tomorrow," he promised Stansson, "we prove it to the world."

21

THREE-RING HOCKEY

The championship game was scheduled to be played in the enormous Anaheim Arena, about thirty miles south of downtown Los Angeles in Orange County. When the Ducks arrived for practice the Anaheim Arena was empty. It was huge—larger than anything the kids could ever have imagined. It was also scary. No one said much. The kids were all thinking the same thing: championship.

Gordon limped onto the ice with his cane. We made it! he thought. He sat down on a bench, and Adam Banks walked over. He held out his hockey stick and rotated it. He smiled proudly, and so did Gordon.

"I woke up this morning and the pain was gone," said Banks. The rest of the team was huddled around them on the bench.

"Adam," Gordon said. "We have a full roster." He looked at Russ, then back at Adam. As much as Adam wanted to play, he knew the team needed the knucklepuck.

Then Charlie stepped forward.

"Banks can have my place," he said. He knew Adam Banks was the better player. "It's what I can do for the team." He turned to his teammate. "Just do your best, Adam."

"Charlie," Gordon said, patting him on the back. "I need you on the bench coaching right there with me."

Charlie smiled. There was no place else he would rather be during the game.

That evening Team USA and Team Iceland stood opposite each other on the ice. It was time.

The arena was packed to capacity with thousands of cheering fans waving flags and holding placards.

Gordon could hardly make himself heard over the noise.

"Okay," Gordon explained to his team at the conclusion of the national anthems. "Here we are. We made it here as a team, we're leaving as a team, right?"

"RIGHT!" shouted the Ducks.

"Now, listen," Gordon reminded them. "I'm standing tall. Forget about yesterday. I don't want to play that way."

"But, Coach, they hurt you," said Portman. The kids all chimed in in support.

Gordon was touched. "Thanks, guys," he said. "That means a lot. But I'm your coach, right? And I say we play fair and beat them good. Real good. Stand tall! Heads up high!"

Pumped up by Gordon's enthusiasm, the kids leaped from the bench, and with a collective roar they hit the ice.

The puck was dropped to begin the first period. Guy controlled the face-off, skated past a defender, and was just about to flip a pass when he was checked hard into the boards by a Viking. The puck ricocheted off the boards and shot like a rocket toward the Team USA net. Goldberg tried clearing the puck behind the net but was tripped by a Vikings player. Dwayne swerved in to cut off the winger, but he was too late. The winger flicked the puck to Olaf. The Ducks recognized him as the Viking who had started the fight on the beach. With Goldberg down on the play, Olaf slapped the puck easily into the net.

Team Iceland jumped out to an early 1–0 lead.

"Too slow, big boy," heckled Olaf as Goldberg got to his feet. Goldberg lunged toward Olaf, but Ken and Dwayne pulled him back.

"No," said Dwayne. "You heard what the coach said."

"Besides," added Ken. "That guy'll kill you."

Goldberg realized instantly that Ken was right.

"Well, at least hold me back like I'm going to kill him," he instructed his friends.

Next, Gordon sent Russ and Jesse onto the ice. Coach Stansson retaliated by sending out two Vikings players to "greet" Russ. No way was Stansson going to allow him an opportunity to shoot his knucklepuck.

When play resumed the Vikings cleverly double-teamed Russ until the ref turned his back. WHAP! Russ went down like a ton of bricks. He groggily climbed to his feet and began moving off the ice. But once he was clear of the Vikings defenders, Russ suddenly swerved and skated at full speed back down the ice toward the loose puck.

The Vikings were caught off guard!

Russ quickly readied himself for a knucklepuck. It looked as if he would have a clear shot on goal. But before he could shoot, two Vikings defenders were on him. In the scuffle the puck squirted free down the ice, and a quick-thinking Vikings player scooped it up and smashed it past Goldberg for another goal.

The scoreboard lit up: Vikings 2, Team USA 0.

Gordon knew that Stansson had ordered the two Vikings to rough up Russ. It was dirty hockey but typical of Stansson. Gordon had to concede one thing: Stansson knew how to play dirty enough to win but clean enough to avoid penalties.

Gordon watched helplessly as the Ducks were overpowered by a succession of cheap shots, hooks, and slashes. He would not order his players to retaliate, however. He wanted to win. But he wanted to win fair.

Gordon turned to Adam Banks. "You're on," he said. "Be careful, Adam."

As soon as Banks was on the ice, a Vikings player closed in on him and began hacking savagely at his wrist. Banks tried twisting away from the defender, but as he broke free Olaf jumped in and brought his stick down hard on Adam's arm.

The ref immediately called a slashing penalty. Olaf smiled as Adam skated slowly off the ice.

With Olaf in the box for a two-minute penalty, Team USA had the power play.

Dwayne was first to control the puck. Almost immediately, however, he was sandwiched by two hulking Vikings defenders. The puck went flying. Gunnar scooped it up and skated toward Goldberg. Luis reached in to deflect the shot but just missed. The puck sliced past Goldberg and into the net.

The buzzer sounded, ending the first period.

Team Iceland had a commanding 3–0 lead.

It became obvious at the beginning of the second period that Team USA's strategy had changed somewhat. Portman and Fulton went after a Viking who had the puck. The two giants spread their arms and clotheslined the smaller Vikings player. He went down hard. The crowd cheered. Team USA was showing some grit, and the crowd loved it.

Gordon turned to Ken on the bench. "Okay, Ken," he said. "You got the protection. Now, remember the double Hamill Camel with the half twist?"

Ken nodded.

"Well, forget the half twist."

When Ken hit the ice, a Vikings player attempted to check him. Ken leaped up and did a full 360-degree turn. He spun magnificently, his arms above his head, his stick twirling in the air.

Startled, three confused Vikings players jumped out of Ken's path. When he came to a slashing stop, Ken was right in front of the Vikings goal. He took a quick pass and sent the puck rattling into the net.

The crowd jumped to its feet and cheered.

Team USA had narrowed the deficit to 3—1.

Triumph turned to tragedy, however, when seconds later an exuberant Portman and Fulton skated down the ice, slapping high-fives with their Team USA teammates. As payback they skated past the Team USA bench to Team Iceland's bench. They slapped all their players, too . . . in the head. The ref immediately pulled them off the ice and threw a major ten-minute penalty on them for unsportsmanlike conduct.

Now it was Team Iceland's turn. On the next play Olaf went after Connie and knocked her roughly to the ground.

"That ain't right," griped Dwayne from the bench. He was steaming.

Olaf turned and grinned when he saw Luis and Guy stampeding toward him. He calmly spread his arms, scarecrow-style, and clotheslined both players to the ground.

Gordon groaned and turned to his players on the bench. "One minute and fifty-nine seconds left in the period," he told them. "Stand tall. Let me see the Flying V."

Jesse skated out ahead of the four others. He got the puck and fell back as his teammates fell into the V formation. Unfortunately, the five Vikings charged them from either side and scattered the Flying V like bowling pins. Gunnar grabbed the puck, broke in alone, and made a quick, clean score.

Gordon sneaked a disgusted look at the Vikings bench. Stansson was beaming. He had made a mockery of the Mighty Ducks' famous Flying V.

Connie had seen enough. Even though she

knew the Vikings were gunning for her, she jumped off the bench and put herself into play. Dwayne tried to stop her, but she wouldn't listen.

On the next play the puck went skidding into a corner. Connie hustled after it. Big Olaf was charging up behind her like a runaway freight train.

"Get out of there, Connie!" shouted Gordon.

"Leave the puck!" screamed Charlie.

Connie couldn't hear them. At the last second she turned and gasped. Olaf was almost upon her. Suddenly a rope came flying through the air. It tightened around Olaf and yanked him to the ground. Cowboy Dwayne had lassoed Olaf!

The fans in the stands reacted with wild cheers. Nevertheless, Dwayne was pulled off the ice for the obvious penalty.

"Two minutes," said the ref. "For . . . er . . . *roping*, I guess."

"This isn't a hockey game," Gordon muttered to himself. "It's a circus."

Mercifully the buzzer sounded to end the second period.

Team Iceland 4, Team USA 1.

22

RETURN OF THE MIGHTY DUCKS

"Did you all enjoy that?" asked Gordon between periods in the locker room.

"YESSSSS!" the kids shouted back.

"Okay," said Gordon. "Well, so did they. Because they're still up by three, and we're one period away from defeat."

Jesse shrugged his shoulders. "If we can't beat them, we might as well keep our pride," he said.

"That's not pride, Jesse," replied Gordon. "Sure, when Dwayne roped Olaf part of me cheered. Believe me, I wanted to cream that guy who busted my knee in the minors, too. And I *really* wanted to get Stansson back." He shook his head slowly. "My knee will heal. But if I become someone I'm not, if I sink to their level, I've lost more than my knee."

The kids looked at each other. Gordon was making sense.

"We're not goons," Gordon reminded them. "We're not bullies. No matter what other people say and do, we have to be ourselves."

Gordon turned to Portman. "You," he said. "Who are you?"

"Uh, Dean Portman."

"From where?"

"Chicago, Illinois."

"Nice to know you." Gordon turned to Julie. "You! Who are you?"

"Julie Gaffney, from Bangor, Maine."

"And don't forget it," said Gordon. He turned again. "You?"

"Luis Mendoza. Miami, Florida."

Gordon turned from one player to the next until he had run through the roster.

"That's right," he said finally. "And I'm Gordon Bombay from Minneapolis, Minnesota. We're Team USA. Gathered from all across America. And we're gonna stick together. Through thick and thin we'll fly together because . . . "

"We're Ducks," said Jan, who had been standing in the doorway.

"That's right," said Gordon. "So, when the wind blows hard and the sky is black?"

"Ducks fly together!" shouted the kids.

"And just when you think you're about to fall apart?" asked Ms. MacKay.

"Ducks fly together!" came the answer.

"When everyone says it can't be done?" asked Gordon.

"DUCKS FLY TOGETHER!"

"Now," said Jan as he walked in from the doorway. "New Ducks and old Ducks must unite under a new banner. I thought perhaps something . . . like this."

Jan slowly opened his coat. He was wearing a new-style Mighty Ducks jersey. The kids roared their approval. Jan brought in two boxes of jerseys. The kids went crazy.

"Win or lose," said Gordon, "we go out like Ducks. Mighty Ducks."

The Mighty Ducks skated out onto the ice to begin the third period. They wore their new jerseys proudly. The crowd cheered wildly when they saw them.

Coach Stansson objected to the uniform change, but according to the rules there was nothing he could do about it. To divert attention from the Ducks, he began to lead the Vikings in their team chant. The Ducks replied by quietly intoning their own, whispering at first, but gradually building it into a loud crescendo of "QUACK!

QUACK! QUACK! QUACK! QUACK! QUACK! QUACK! QUACK!" The audience enthusiastically joined in, drowning out the Vikings chant.

The stunt had apparently worked. Team Iceland seemed to have lost its concentration. Following the initial face-off in the third period, Portman scored an easy goal. Just like that, it was Vikings 4, Ducks 2.

But just as suddenly the Vikings struck back. Goldberg made a great save on a hard shot but bobbled the puck. It skipped loose in front of the net, and a Viking swept in and flipped it home. The Vikings had regained their three-goal lead.

Gordon called time-out and gathered his team on the bench. They looked beat. Gordon had to do something to get the fire back. But what?

Charlie, as assistant coach, had been observing the Vikings for weaknesses since the game began. He quickly improvised a play on the blackboard. Gordon studied it and looked impressed.

"Check it out, guys," said Gordon.

The kids studied the play.

"No way, man," said Averman. The play involved some rather unusual stunts. "It'll never work. This isn't the NBA."

"It's the perfect teamwork play," insisted Charlie. "It can work. I know it."

Everyone turned to Gordon.

"It's Charlie's call," said the coach.

Charlie smiled. "Go for it!" he said.

Gordon ordered a line change. Averman, Banks, Jesse, Luis, and Dwayne took up their positions on the ice. Dwayne skated behind the Team USA net, took the puck, and sent a quick pass to Jesse. A Viking charged him. Jesse flipped the puck to Luis. By this time Dwayne had skated to center ice. Two Vikings defenders closed in on him as Luis sent Dwayne the puck.

The Ducks, however, had followed Charlie's instructions to the letter. It was time for the final move.

"Now!" shouted Charlie from the bench.

Dwayne swung at the puck like a golfer. The puck sailed almost straight up into the air and nearly hit the scoreboard before it fell back onto the ice.

It landed right in front of Portman, who smashed it into the Vikings net.

Now it was Vikings 5, Ducks 3.

There were two minutes left in the final period.

Two minutes left in the game.

Two minutes left to their dream. On the following face-off Luis found himself on open ice heading toward the Vikings net. If he could get the puck, he thought, he could score an easy goal! Then he panicked. He wasn't very good at stopping. What if he bungled the play by crashing into the boards, or another player, or the net?

He knew he had to try. A teammate had already spotted him and was preparing to shovel him the puck. As he flew down the ice he concentrated on a spot a few feet in front of the goal. He *had* to make a clean stop.

All of a sudden he came to a slashing halt. Ice showered down all around him. He had not fallen! He was standing straight. Luis was so pleased with himself, he momentarily forgot about the puck, which had slid to a stop at his feet.

"PUT IT IN!" shouted Gordon frantically from the bench. "THE PUCK! PUT IT IN!"

Luis slapped at the puck. SCORE!

The crowd roared again.

The Ducks were only one goal down!

Gordon pumped his fist into the air. He could feel it. Just one more, he thought. Gordon smiled when he saw Stansson stampeding angrily back and forth on the bench. He was so mad, he was throwing hockey sticks and banging the walls.

Gordon turned to his players on the bench. It was time to deliver the knockout, his expression said. "Russ," he ordered. "You're on."

Russ smiled and skated out onto the ice. Stansson countered by immediately sending out three Vikings to cover him. They played Russ so tight he could hardly breathe. "Chill," he complained to a defender. "I don't even have the puck."

"And it will stay that way," the player answered grimly.

Gordon saw what was happening and called time-out. He motioned Russ back to the bench. He glanced over to see Stansson, who was smiling. Gordon huddled the players, then sent them back onto the ice.

Stansson grinned. Gordon had pulled Russ. Obviously he believed he had outwitted Gordon by triple-teaming his star player.

But the triumphant grin slid from Stansson's face when he could not see Russ on the Team USA bench. Where had he gone?

Meanwhile, the Ducks seemed to have trouble getting the puck out of their own zone. It almost looked as if they weren't even trying.

"NOW!" Gordon suddenly shouted to his players.

Immediately Jesse passed the puck to Goldberg. When Goldberg took the puck, however, he ripped off his mask. It wasn't Goldberg at all—but *Russ*!

Russ tossed away the goalie stick. At the same time, Jesse threw him his shooting stick. Russ whacked one of his famous knucklepucks. The puck hurtled across the ice toward the Vikings goalie. The players froze as they watched the puck wobble in a crazy arc toward the net. The goalie dropped into a crouch, but at the last second the puck seemed to stall out. The goalie put up his glove. And the puck took a quick dip and slid just under it. Score, Team USA.

The buzzer sounded, ending regulation play.

The Ducks had tied the game, 5—5.

The arena erupted into pandemonium.

The ref skated over to both benches to explain what would happen next.

"International rules means it goes to a shoot-out. Five players on breakaways. Most goals win."

Gordon turned to his team and picked his best five: Dwayne, Guy, Jesse, Fulton and . . .

He pointed to Banks.

"I don't know, Coach," said Banks, hesitating. His wrist had healed, but he worried that he might not have full motion control.

"I do," said Gordon. "You're in."

The five Ducks skated out onto the ice. Meanwhile, Stansson sent out his five best.

Jesse got the first shot. He took a breath, skated smoothly on goal, then let fly with a confident slap shot. The puck slammed straight into the net.

There was a cheer from the crowd. It was 1—0, Team USA.

Now it was Team Iceland's turn. Their player circled around the puck, then roared with it across the ice and shot. The puck zoomed past Goldberg and into the net: 1—1.

Guy was up next. He looked over at the bench

to Connie, who smiled. Guy shot and scored. It was now 2—1.

The next Vikings player tried to score with a deke. But Goldberg saw it coming and made a brilliant save. The Ducks were one goal ahead!

Dwayne pushed the puck ahead of him and glided toward the goal. At the last second he played a backhand deke. The Vikings goalie didn't fall for it, however. He stopped the puck cold.

Olaf lumbered up to the puck next. Instead of maneuvering toward the goal, he tried to overpower Goldberg with a cannon shot. It worked. The score was tied: 2—2.

It was Fulton's turn. He reared back and sent the puck screaming. The puck went flying toward the goal. The Vikings goalie didn't even make an attempt at a save. The only save he was interested in was the one on his life. He dove to the side as the puck smashed against the back of the net: 3—2, Team USA!

Goldberg nearly made a terrific save on the next shot, but he was caught off balance and lost control of the puck. It bobbled out of his glove and trickled into the net.

The score was tied. Each team had one shot left.

It was all up to Adam Banks.

Banks skated in front of the puck. He flexed his wrist one last time. His heart was pounding as he bore down on the puck. The slashing of his skates echoed through the arena as he glided the puck across the ice. Instinct told Adam to deke. He faked once, twice, three times. Then he did something unexpected. He faked again! The Vikings goalie had committed one way, and Adam went the other. He pushed the blade of his stick forward and skipped the puck smoothly into the net.

The roar from the crowd was like an explosion. They jumped from their seats and cheered wildly. One play to go, and the championship would be decided.

"Julie," Gordon called down to the bench. "You've got the fast glove side. I know this kid's move. Triple deke glove side. Anticipate it and you got him."

Gordon recognized the final Vikings player and knew that he played with a sleek, slippery style. Goldberg was big and strong but wasn't that fast.

"What if he goes stick side?" asked Julie.

"He's fancy. He'll go glove. Don't hesitate."

Averman leaned forward. "How can you be so sure?" he asked Gordon.

"I'm the coach," Gordon answered. "I've studied the players. It's our best shot."

Julie skated out to the net, high-fiving Goldberg as he headed back to the bench.

From behind his mask Gunnar smirked. They

were sending a girl out to face him down, he thought. Did they *want* to lose?

The ref gave Gunnar the signal to begin play. Once again silence descended over the arena. It was as if no one even dared take a breath. Julie hunched and waited.

Finally, Gunnar skated toward the net. Julie calmly counted his dekes.

One . . .

Too soon to predict, Julie thought, her eyes glued to Gunnar.

Two . . .

It could go either way.

Three!

Julie lunged right, committing to Gunnar's glove side.

Gunnar shot the puck. She had guessed right! She lunged for the puck and felt a slap as it hit her glove. She went down face first onto the ice.

Julie slowly opened the glove and smiled. She fished the puck out of her glove and tossed it back onto the ice.

The game was over. Once again the Ducks had done the impossible. They were champions!

The audience cheered madly.

Gordon, Jan, Ms. MacKay, and the rest of the players all ran out onto the ice in celebration.

A throng of reporters mobbed Gordon, asking thousands of questions.

Adam Banks looked up into the stands. Two scouts had put away their notebooks and risen from their seats. They began to applaud. Banks smiled.

A representative from the Goodwill Committee skated out holding the American flag. He gave it to Banks. The flag was passed through the hands of every Ducks player.

Gordon was standing with his arm around Michele when a reporter broke in.

"Gordon Bombay," said the reporter. "You just coached Team USA to the gold against all odds. What are you going to do now?"

"We're going home," he replied.

Then he looked at Michele and smiled.

23

THE MIGHTY DUCKS
OF ANAHEIM

The next day Gordon, Jan, Michele, and the team
were waiting in the departure terminal at Los Angeles International Airport for the plane that
would take them home.

Finally, the announcement came, and the group
headed toward the gate.

"Ducks!" came a familiar voice. "Ducks! Wait!"

They turned. Don Tibbles was running toward
them.

"I have news," he announced breathlessly.
"Great news! I got a job with the new NHL fran-
chise in Anaheim. The owners saw the final game.
They really like your style."

"Well, great," said Gordon.

"No," said Tibbles. "I mean they *really* liked
your style. And your colors, too! They're going to
call themselves the Mighty Ducks!"

Everyone looked at each other. They were astounded. The Ducks in the NHL?

"But they can't do it unless they have your approval," said Tibbles. "They want to be Ducks."

Gordon looked at his players.

"Team," he asked. "What do you say?"

The Ducks looked at each other and nodded. "QUAAAAACKKK!" They shouted their approval in unison.

Gordon said his final good-byes to Tibbles and led the team onto the plane. As he took his seat, Gordon wondered what the future held for him. Of one thing he was certain: Even though his knee was completely healed, his days in the minor leagues were over. He was too old for that. But hockey was his life.

He smiled and leaned back into his seat. He would just have to figure out how to keep it that way.